LYNNE WAITE CHAPMAN

Secret Mercy
Small Town Mystery, Book 2

By Lynne Waite Chapman

Copyright © 2023 by Lynne Waite Chapman
Published by Gordian Books, an imprint of Winged Publications
Cover design by Cynthia Hickey

This book is a work of fiction. Names, characters, places, and incidents are the product of the author's imagination and are used fictitiously. Any resemblance to actual events, locales, or persons, living or dead, is coincidental.

All rights reserved including the right to reproduce this book or portions thereof in any form whatsoever – except short passages for reviews – without express permission.

ISBN-13: **979-8-8690-8018-9**

Prologue

Twin Fawn, a small town in southern Indiana boasted a population of around a thousand citizens. The majority of those souls had passed the age of fifty-five. City officials and realtors would argue those statistics when touting the promise of new growth in the community. Snowfall measured only an average of fifteen inches per year, but cold weather often set in by late October.

It was on an October evening that one old woman, Willow Ottenweller, wrapped her arms around herself and shivered. The wind whistled through leaky windows. Her son, Johnny, had pressed her to replace those windows. Sure, replace them, and then what would be next? In her experience, one repair always led to another and then another. Young people would never understand the limits of a budget. The old mansion, her home, had stood in Twin Fawn for a hundred and fifty years. At least that's what she'd been told. She guessed the place might have been older than that. She knew her birth had taken place in the upstairs bedroom more than eighty years ago. The sturdy old building would last a while longer.

Willow selected an old hand knitted sweater from the closet and buttoned it up to her neck. The wind howled but at least it was sure to strip the remainder of the leaves from the old oak tree. Just as well. She could get them raked up before the snow came.

She took her tea to the window to watch the swaying trees illuminated by moonlight. Clouds pushed along by the breeze blocked the soft light at intervals. Crazy shadows raced across the yard from the south to north.

Except for one. That disoriented shadow lurched across the lawn to the east. It didn't seem to find its source in any cloud.

Could there be an intruder sculking about in her yard? Somone stupid enough to brave this unpleasant weather? She'd had but a glimpse. From the looks of him, he stood tall and muscular. And he walked with an odd gate. Sort of a lope. Was one foot dragging? He must be lame. These were traits to remember, should she decide to notify the police of his trespass.

And how to describe the moaning? An unearthly sound. Not the howling of the wind through ancient window casings. Something else. Something almost, but not quite, human.

Willow laughed at herself. Surely it was a silly old woman's imagination.

But still.

The wail sounded again, sending a chill from her backbone through her shoulders. No. This was something that could not be blamed on the storm. Willow shifted the curtain across the window. She clutched her tea cup and sat in her old rocking chair, drawing a blanket around her. Then she set the chair to rocking. The creaking of the old wood had always irritated Johnny. Not that it bothered him as a baby, when the rocking would lull him to sleep. Later, he'd complained he couldn't hear his television program for the squeaking. It had never been annoying to Willow. She considered it comforting evidence of permanence. Some old things were meant to be kept and treasured.

Yet, try as it might, the scraping of the wood didn't quite drown out the dreadful keening resonating from outside on this bleak night.

Chapter One

I dragged a thick woolen scarf around my neck and tightened the collar of my jacket. The weatherman had predicted chilly and breezy conditions, but the sun was shining brightly. I looked forward to the brisk walk to work. How many more opportunities would I have to leave the car at home? Only five blocks to work. I craved the exercise. Or my forty-year-old body did. I just loved a walk in the park, even with plants going into hibernation for the season and trees losing their leaves. Once at work I would be stuck sitting at a desk for most of the day looking at dust on the cabinets and walls in need of paint.

But first, I had to do something about the garbage cans rolling about in the street. The wind gusts had been powerful overnight. Good citizen as I am, I grabbed the can and pulled it to the side of the street, then chased down another. After I'd finished my clean-up campaign, I continued my walk.

I arrived at Bennett's Hardware, my workplace, grateful to get in out of the chill that had begun to filter its way through my coat. "Good morning, Mr. Bennett."

My boss stood at the sales counter wearing white shirt and tan slacks, his uniform for almost every day since I'd known him. Now that the cold weather had set in, he'd added a blue striped pullover sweater. His attire for the winter.

"Good morning, Libby. Did I see that you walked to work this morning? Car trouble?"

"No, my car's fine. I felt like walking today. The sun's shining and it isn't terribly cold. I want to take advantage of as many days as possible before the mornings are freezing." To be truthful, my car's engine had been making a clicking sound, but I was sure it was nothing. I'd take it to a mechanic later, sometime.

Mr. Bennett continued. "Let me know when you're finished today. I'll give you a lift home."

Like many sixty-ish men, when my boss gets an idea in his head, he doesn't really listen to me. "I'll be fine walking. It's supposed to be a nice day."

"Might rain."

"The weather man didn't call for any participation." We'd had this argument so many times that I'd stopped paying attention, too.

Mr. Bennett walked into the store room. I hung my jacket on the hook in the office and slid into my seat at the desk. While the computer booted, I gathered and stacked the receipts from the previous day. The man would simply toss them haphazardly onto the desk when he closed up in the evening, trusting that I'd sort everything out when I arrived the next day. What would Stanley Bennett do without me?

~~

Bennett's Hardware front door flew open with a bang and a gust of cold air.

I'd just taken a much-needed break from balancing inventory against purchase receipts and leaned on the sales counter waiting for the coffee pot to finish brewing. I was a bit surprised to see the diminutive woman who stomped into the store.

A longtime customer, Willow Ottenweller had always seemed a tranquil soul. Strong and energetic for her age, but generally calm. Before this particular episode, I would have described her as a sweet little lady who could warm your heart with her smile and who loved to talk.

She wore over-sized cold weather boots. I thought they might have belonged to her son in his teen years. The calf-length skirt of her dress showed under a longish sweater. A winter coat hung almost to her knees. Her wispy white hair had never been in complete control, but on this day, it failed to behave at all. Tufts stood out in the back, and the sides spread out like butterfly wings. The woman looked like she'd had a rough morning.

I called a greeting. "It's good to see you, Willow. How about some coffee? I have a fresh pot brewing."

She threw a wild-eyed glance in my direction. "I'm sorry, what is your name?"

"It's Liberty Cassell, Katherine Cassell's daughter."

"Oh yes, Liberty. I'm sorry. I've been distracted this morning."

"No problem, Mrs. Ottenweller. How about that coffee?"

"No. No thank you. I don't want any."

She did seem distraught. More upset than I'd ever seen her. It was likely best to leave her alone. We all have our bad days.

The tiny woman continued her stalk down the aisle. I figured if she wanted my help, she would let me know. I've never been an aggressive salesperson. Actually, not a salesperson at all. An accountant of sorts. I kept the books for the store. I ventured onto the sales floor only when the four walls of my little office became oppressive.

Mr. Bennett, having witnessed her entrance, hustled out from the back room. "Hello Willow. It's so nice to see you." My boss could be very kind to our older customers. "I sense something is bothering you. What may I help you with?"

She had been so distracted that he stood at her side before she noticed him. She jerked her head up to gaze at Mr. Bennett. "A lock. I need a big heavy lock for my shed. And what do you have that will secure the lid of my garbage can?"

Willow scooted past my boss before he had a chance to offer any suggestion, and continued pacing the aisles. She selected multiple items only to hold them in her hand for a moment and then discard them—out of place. She destroyed our organized products while carrying on a continuous whispered conversation with no one in particular. This seemed odd behavior even for Twin Fawn residents, and it was making a mess of the display shelves that I'd helped to arrange.

I'd always considered Willow Ottenweller level-headed for her age. She'd never been a problem in the few times I'd waited on her at Bennett's Hardware. I guessed her to be in her eighties. I suppose mental episodes might come on quickly for the aged.

Mr. Bennett took his time following a few steps

behind Willow. One thing I admired about my boss was his patience. He considered it his responsibility to cater to the emotional needs of his customers while supplying nuts and bolts. So, he walked behind her occasionally restoring an item to its rightful place.

He spoke softly. "Tell me what's on your mind, Willow."

I wouldn't have been so calm, but I guess he'd built up a bank of experience dealing with some of the odd residents of our little town. He was closer to Willow's age. Not as old, but maybe had more understanding of quirks of the elderly.

"We probably have something that will fit the shed, but I'm not sure about the garbage can. What's going on? Are the raccoons giving you trouble? They're pesky creatures."

Willow glanced toward the front door and then at me. I pretended to be intrigued with the cash register. As if I hadn't even noticed her tirade.

She glanced up and down the aisle before she said, "No, not raccoons. It's the Crosley Monster."

Monster? My head snapped up so fast I worried about whiplash. After that, it was obvious I'd been eavesdropping.

In his kind way of addressing everyone, no matter how skewed their thoughts, Mr. Bennett said, "The Crosley Monster? That's interesting. I've always thought of it as a myth." He lifted his shoulders. "You know how people love to talk and make up tall stories."

Willow huffed and aimed beady blue eyes at him. "People. They're just like my boy, Johnny."

I'd met Johnny Ottenweller, Willow's son. He was not a boy. He was probably going on fifty, at least. Not bad looking, with white hair like Willow's though cut short and controlled.

His business and family home were located a couple of counties away, but he made regular trips to Twin Fawn to check on his mother. He'd been in the store several times with her. There was always something that needed fixing at Willow's house, so they'd make a trip to the hardware. He seemed to be a nice loving son who catered to his mom whenever he could.

Willow wasn't feeling the love at the moment. She grumbled, "He didn't believe me either. I called him first thing this morning, because I needed to talk to him. Don't mind telling you I was scared. I didn't get a bit of sleep all night. Just like a man to dismiss it. Did he care anything about what I felt? No! Didn't even give me a chance to tell him what I saw."

Mr. Bennett leaned toward Willow. "Maybe you caught Johnnie at a bad time. Possibly before he'd had his coffee. And you know, for someone who has never seen it, the Crosley Monster might be hard to take seriously."

Willow turned angry eyes at Mr. Bennett, again. "Of course, the monster's real. People tell stories about it, but that doesn't mean those tales aren't based on fact. And as for no one seeing it, there's a report that it was seen not that long ago. My neighbor Luann told me. I think it was back in 2006. Chased a group of hikers right out of the Crosley Wild Life Area."

Johnnie may not have been interested, but Willow had grabbed my attention. I quit trying to look busy and moved a couple aisles closer to Willow and Mr. Bennett.

When the old woman twisted toward me, her cloud of cotton-like hair floating in the breeze, she seemed sad and alone. "You know about the Crosley Monster, don't you?"

"Um. I'm afraid not." She wanted confirmation, but I considered honesty the best policy. And it would be hard to fake it when I had no idea what she was talking about.

Willow stretched to her full height—about four foot nothing—and raised her voice to an authoritative level. "I've studied 'em. Likely a relative of the Sasquatch. Big and muscular. They walk upright on two feet. People say they can be at least eight feet tall and covered with hair. Nobody knows how many might live in Crosley Forest. I'm certain there's at least one family unit."

Willow turned and gazed through the front window. "They could live right here in Twin Fawn. Probably out in the country. That'd be a good place to hide."

The woman had my full attention. Not that I believed her. As Mr. Bennett said, it was a tall tale. But I wanted to hear her story. "You say they're tall and hairy? Like a gorilla? Is the hair very long?" Mr. Bennett shifted his eyes to me. A clear message for me to refrain from encouraging her.

But I've always loved scary stories.

"Like a gorilla, but shaped more like a man. They tend to have long arms. Longer than a man would have. Some people say they're a cross between an ape and a sloth. Isn't that something? I'm not sure about the length of the hair."

"What color is it—the hair?" Don't ask me why I

was fascinated with the hair.

Willow's heart rate must've been soaring as she related her tale. Her eyes were big and round. Her cheeks flushed. "All the stories say that the color ranges from blond to light brown to black."

Mr. Bennett gave me another look that I interpreted as, 'Shut up.' *You would think I'd heed his meaningful looks, as often as they'd been directed at me.*

He turned his attention back to Willow, keeping his tone soft and comforting. "I've heard the stories, but that's in Crosley not Twin Fawn."

For such a tiny woman, Willow could stand her ground. "Crosley Lake isn't particularly far away. A creature of that size could easily migrate over here. Just a day's walk, maybe two, depending on whether there were little ones with it."

My boss is resilient. He tried changing lanes. "You say you've had trouble with your garbage can?"

Willow's head bobbed in a nod. "I suppose the monster, or monsters, worked up quite a hunger on the trip. You know, out of its element. I imagine there aren't enough fish and small animals to satisfy that kind of appetite here in Twin Fawn. Especially if there's a family of them."

Mr. Bennett pulled off his glasses and propped them on his almost bald head, but remained silent. He was at a loss for words or had given up on Willow's sanity.

She planted fists on her hips. "I wouldn't want the creatures hurt, but the authorities need to find a way to round 'em up and get them back to a safer place. Back at the park. So, I called the police. That Officer Arnie wouldn't even listen to me. Too busy, he said. I guess there's some kind of thefts and destruction on North Point Avenue."

Willow locked eyes with me. "Mark my words, Liberty. You have to stand up for yourself in this world. When you get old, nobody listens to you. Just wait until Arnie starts getting reports from all over town. It was my yard last night. Hard telling who's next. There are bound to be more sightings. Just you wait."

She glanced around the store. "I'll take that big padlock for my shed, but I don't see anything to protect my trash can. Guess I'll keep the can in the shed." Willow grabbed the lock and made her way to the cash register.

I hurried to beat Mr. Bennett to the cash register and grabbed the lock. "What convinced you it was the Crosley Monster?"

"Didn't I tell you? I heard the moan. Not the howl people talked about." She lowered her voice and leaned toward me. "Never heard anything like it. An unearthly moan. Bone chilling." She shivered. "Combined with a growl."

Unearthly moan with growl undertones? Yikes, seems like she could have led with that piece of information. "You say it was unlike anything you'd ever heard?"

"Yep. When I looked out the window, I saw the creature leaving the yard. It was dark out but I got a glimpse. Light colored hair kind of reflected in the street lights. Guess you'd call it blonde. I bet it's real pretty in daylight."

Willow leaned on the counter. "I didn't sleep all night and went out to the yard as soon as it got light. I found the footprints. They were hard to make out in the grass, but I knew what to look for and they were there." Willow stood for a moment before she went on. "And my garbage can was thrown clear across the yard." She glanced at Mr. Bennett, who had gone back to arranging the shelves. "There's no way a raccoon did that." She picked up her package. "I'm thinking of getting a ball bat. You don't have any of those, do you?"

I shook my head. "No bats here but you can probably find one at the sport shop."

"Don't want to get a gun, but I need something for protection in case it tries to get inside." At this, Willow marched out of the store.

Mr. Bennett glanced at the banging door and shook his head. "Silly old woman. She's lived alone for too long."

I'd never noticed any hint of dementia in Willow, but I guess it's a sneaky disease. Had to agree with her though. People don't always listen to older women. Eventually I'd join that unfortunate group, losing credibility as we age.

"You don't believe her, then?"

Mr. Bennett laughed. "An eight-foot-tall, hairy monster in Twin Fawn? And blond at that?" He guffawed. "Must have been to the beauty shop. Don't tell me you fell for that nonsense." Mr. Bennett picked up his clipboard and began checking off items in the new delivery. "Like I said, she has lived alone for too long. Probably rattles around in that big ancient house of hers. It's the one beside the park."

"The old mansion across from Bird Song Park? I've admired it on my walks through the park. Never connected it with Willow."

"That's the one. Not many would call it a mansion. It's a big old house. I can't imagine how she cares for it. She should sell it. Her son wants her to. Told me so last time he was in, but she's fighting him on it. It would be an easy sale. The town council even offered to buy it. They have plans to tear it down and extend the park. Wouldn't that be nice for the town? Getting rid of an eyesore and gaining a play area for the kids." Mr. Bennett gazed into the distance. "Maybe a water feature."

Willow's home did need some attention. The wraparound porch had lost some of the decorative corner pieces. The window casings appeared loose. But I admired the original architecture. "I wouldn't call it an eyesore. I'd say it has character. The culmination of years of family moments." I've always been fascinated with old buildings. "A larger park area might be good for Twin Fawn, but wouldn't you hate to see her pressured into giving up her home if she doesn't want to?"

Mr. Bennett grasped his clipboard with both hands. I had the feeling a lecture was coming. "There comes a time for everyone when it isn't safe for them to live alone. Experiencing hallucinations of a big hairy monster is a pretty strong indication, wouldn't you say? Willow's time has come."

"I see your point. Poor Willow must have been scared to death all night."

Mr. Bennett put his glasses back on his nose and carried his clipboard to the store room. He called over his shoulder. "I sure hope she doesn't get herself a gun."

Well, I couldn't argue with him. After all, what

was worse than an old lady in the progression of dementia stumbling around in an old, unkempt mansion? One carrying a gun.

Chapter Two

How much time had I wasted listening to monster stories? Back at my desk, I searched for the stopping point in my figures. Where had I left off? "Darn it!" I slapped the desk, creating more of a ruckus than I'd planned.

Mr. Bennett passed by the office and paused, lifting his eyebrows. "Are you okay in there?"

"I was out there for coffee, when Willow came in. Then I got so engrossed in her story I forgot it. I haven't had my coffee, and now I've lost my place in the receipts." I shoved my chair back and jogged to the coffee maker.

"I'd counted on getting off work a little early." My mother's weekly Bible study night gave me time to myself with no arguing over the television.

Good old Stanley Bennett. "Don't worry about it. Go ahead and take off. All that paperwork will still be here tomorrow." Yes, my work would wait for me and there would be more. Mr. Bennett was kind, but didn't help my work ethic. Slacking off was a big enough temptation without encouragement from the boss.

I filled my cup, and with a fresh injection of

caffeine, dug in and finished my work without further interruption. No more stories about Sasquatch or the Crosley Monster. Or whatever inhabited Willow's nightmare. I'd be willing to bet the poor woman had come to her senses not long after she'd left the hardware store. She'd exhausted all the pent-up stress by ranting to us and regained her sanity. Still, it had made for an interesting morning at the store. Her crazy story had relieved the monotony of checks and balances.

Monotony. If my father had heard me, he'd have felt obligated to remind me of those who had no job. Don't ask me why I chose bookkeeping as an occupation. It seemed to be the logical, safe choice at the time, since my mother, Katherine Cassell, served as the librarian and my father, Gerald Cassell, a mail carrier. I've always been good with math. I wanted to serve and be loved by the citizens of Twin Fawn, just like my parents. At the moment, I can't imagine a more tedious occupation than bookkeeping. I'm a people person. Not the super out-going type like my mother, but the type who likes to be around warm bodies. So why am sitting in a dusty office at Bennett's Hardware?

Why not find a more stimulating career? I'd been asked the question and I pondered it occasionally. The first obstacle would be breaking the news to Stanley Bennett. Such a good man. Very easy to work for. I'm just not thrilled with staring at numbers all day, every day.

Leaving would also require some initiative on my part. It would entail finding other employment and I haven't a clue as to what it would be. My mother changed careers recently. She left the library to become a private detective. You can bet that shocked a lot of people, me included. Obviously, she has the ingenuity in the family.

So, this is why I live in the little village of Twin Fawn. It's easy. Most people are nice to me. Cost of living isn't bad. Though not an exciting occupation, the hardware store pays enough to be comfortable. I've been told I'm a small-footprint person. I'm not sure what that means, but if it's that I don't require much, that's me.

Nobody in this town has asked me why I'm not more enterprising. Even my best friend Clair accepts me, just the way I am. If you're looking for ambition, that's Clair. Enterprising, too. She moved into town with her husband, the veterinarian, a few years back and has already built a thriving real estate business. Yet, she still finds time for our coffee talks. We can be found at The Caffeinated Cup almost every day. She works on her phone and laptop while I relax and people watch.

I finished my work and said goodbye to Mr. Bennett by early afternoon. It took a little time to convince him I didn't require a lift. I liked walking.

On my way, I cut over a block and stopped at Twin Fawn's Family Market. The practically empty parking lot assured me of a quick trip picking up a few essential items. I'd begun meandering through the aisles when a cheery voice called my name. It was my neighbor Linda Carlisle. She worked as a checker at the market several days a week. Said she needed to fill up her time since her twins left for college.

I waved and went about my shopping. When I finished, I guided my cart into Linda's lane.

"Hi neighbor. How's Ron?" Her husband had retired recently and of course spent a lot more time at home. Possibly another reason for Linda's part time job.

"He's fine. He's been on a fishing trip with his brother but should be home tonight. I thought I'd enjoy the time alone, but now I can't wait for him to get home."

"The house must seem empty."

She nodded. "It does, and you never know what might be creeping around outside."

Linda rang up the last of my groceries and whispered while we bagged them. "Did you hear?"

I whispered, too. "Um, I guess not. What is it?"

Her voice trembled as she hissed, "A Bigfoot has been sighted right here in Twin Fawn."

I wanted to laugh, but a closer look into those worried eyes convinced me she was dead serious. Gossip spread fast in our little town. I searched for a reply that wouldn't offend her and came up with the brilliant one-word question. "Bigfoot?"

Linda nodded, while she continued bagging groceries. "Willow Ottenweller saw it on her property."

She took a deep breath and glanced down the aisle as more shoppers joined the line. "Can't talk now. My manager's coming. But there's one of those monsters right here in Twin Fawn. Willow saw it, and we don't live very far from her. It would be a quick trip from her house to our neighborhood." She began handing me my bags of groceries, and with a meaningful stare said, "Bolt your doors and be careful if you go out at night. In fact, I wouldn't go out after dark at all." With that she turned her attention to the next in line.

As often happens, I'd purchased more groceries than planned. And hadn't thought about the car sitting at home. I stumbled out of the store, with three bags of smaller items looped over my left arm, a bagged cabbage on my right, and a carton of milk hugged to my chest. Once I got everything balanced, I spent the trek home considering how one little old lady's bad dream was apt to cause mass hysteria in a small town. The panic concerned me more than the possibility of Bigfoot stomping on my petunias.

By the time I'd arrived home and the groceries were sprawled across the kitchen counter, I'd put all monster nonsense out of my mind, again. My mother stepped into the kitchen from the laundry room, holding a hand towel. She'd been living with me since getting kicked out of Clairmont Retirement Village. Not my mom's fault. She just led a more exciting life than the other residents were used to. I guess she made them nervous. And the management hadn't bargained for dealing with a bunch of hysterical old people. I didn't blame them. I'm sure the residents never expected to be roused in the night by gunfire and police sirens. But that is another story.

"Liberty, you're home early. How was your day?"

"A typical day at the hardware. What could be more exciting than guessing whether Mr. Bennett will manage to finish the daily crossword before lunch?"

My mother had a soft, melodic chuckle. "There's something to be said for a day lacking excitement. Twin Fawn is comfortable and quiet." I knew better. My mother pretended to prefer tranquility but recently would jump at any opportunity offering adventure.

She put up an index finger. "Here's some

smalltown excitement for you. I was sitting out on the porch to get a little sun when this little white dog went streaking across the lawn. He was running as fast as his little legs could carry him." She giggled. "Then, a minute later, George Trainer, the guy who owns the car lot on Elm Street, came chasing after it. Right across the lawn, running as fast as he could go, too. If you remember George, he's kind of plump in stature and isn't particularly speedy." This last part brought on a full-blown laugh.

"I bet that was a sight. Was it George's dog?"

"Haven't a clue. The man was in no condition to stop and chat."

I stored the milk and butter in the refrigerator and glanced back at my mother. Knowing she would get a kick out of Willow's story I thought I might as well share it with her. "There was one thing that interrupted the monotony of my day. Willow Ottenweller came in raving about monsters. She thought she saw one in her yard."

Mom finished folding the towel and planted her hands on her hips. "Monsters? Tell me more."

I nodded. "She must have been watching too many late-night documentaries. Sounded like she'd had a nightmare about Sasquatch and thought it was real. She seems to think there's something akin to Bigfoot roaming the streets of Twin Fawn. She insisted one visited her yard last night."

"The poor thing. That probably terrified her."

"I think it did at first. She said she didn't sleep all night. But at the store, she was not so much frightened as planning to go to war with it. She came to the hardware looking for heavy locks to secure her shed and wanted to fasten the lids on her garbage cans. And she thought about getting a baseball bat." I leaned against the counter and twirled a cabbage. "Even if Bigfoot existed, and we know it doesn't, why would it be hanging around in Indiana? Only corn and soy bean fields here. Aren't the Sasquatch supposed to be in Washington state and maybe up in Canada?"

My mother turned toward me and refolded the towel in her hand. "Actually, there have been many sightings reported in other states as well. And Willow is correct about the possibility of them residing here in the Midwest. There are stories about a hairy ape-like creature showing up in several places in Indiana. And many of those sightings were right over in Crosley Fish and Wildlife Area."

"Crosley? That's what Willow was talking about. The Crosley Monster. The park isn't very far from here. Why haven't I heard stories of the monster before?"

"No dear, it isn't far. I suppose you haven't heard of it because the last publicized sightings were back in the 1930's. There has been some talk of it since, but I guess it's never been news-worthy enough to hit the papers."

"So, big hairy ape-like creatures are supposed to be wandering Indiana. No wonder Willow is having nightmares. And now she's telling everyone there's a monster in Twin Fawn. She even had Linda, at the market, spooked."

Mother raised her shoulders. "The stories could be true. Maybe not the monster, but something. I've heard it described as a giant sloth-like creature. Others say it's an ape. I suppose whatever they saw had long arms and lots of hair."

She paused a moment. "And not only sightings. People say they've heard howls in the woods that would curl your hair. Those who have seen it guess it to be at least eight feet tall." She put her palm to her forehead and looked toward the hallway. "I think I may even have a picture."

I slanted my eyes at my mother. "What? You have a picture of Big Foot." My world was collapsing around me. "Where would you get such a thing?"

My mother twisted toward me. "Lorin Sanderson gave it to me years ago."

I should have known. Lorin Sanderson was another elderly Twin Fawn resident. Probably as old and as crazy as Willow.

My mother went on. "One day he told me about it and said his kids wanted to throw it away. He thought it was important so I promised I'd keep it for him. I stashed it away in my jewelry box and forgot about it. It's been there for years. Wait." She left the kitchen and eventually returned to hand me a worn newspaper clipping.

The paper was crinkled, and the black and white fuzzy photograph took some concentration. At first all I could make out where trees.

Following my mother's index finger, I found the shadowed figure partially hidden by vegetation. It looked like a large ape, or possibly a very tall man. Or a tall bush. "That's it? It's far away and not very clear."

"Well, dear. I doubt the Crosley Monster would want to get close to the public." She winked. "He'd be posing for pictures all the time. Then people would want to take selfies with him and probably ask for autographs. Can you imagine? Very disturbing."

A joke. I laughed and went about my work. "Oh, thank goodness. For a minute there I thought you really bought in to that stuff."

Mom smiled and returned to folding laundry. "I need to finish this and catch up on my Bible study."

I stood beside the refrigerator. "You don't buy into it. Do you?"

She called from the laundry room. "Do you think I'm crazy?"

~~

"Make way, I'm coming through." My mother placed her hands on my shoulders and gently scooted me to the side as she trotted through the living room. I knew better than to stand in the middle of the narrow passageway between the sofa and the recliner when Katherine Cassell was on a mission. She grabbed her Bible and notebook from the end table, shoving them into her flowered backpack on her way past. "I'm late, and I'll get some raised eyebrows if I walk in after discussion has begun. Charity's a stickler for promptness." Charity, the new pastor's wife, didn't want to give anyone the excuse that the study group took too much time out of their day. "We start right on time and finish one hour later, on the dot."

Mom paused to zip her backpack. "I'm actually glad she insists on keeping a schedule. You know how some women's study groups run on for hours and never get to the meat of the Scripture. With Charity in charge, we finish our study and then have a chance to stay and talk if we want."

No, I didn't know how other women's groups worked, and Mom knew this. To her consternation, I'd never progressed past my daily devotional. Not to worry, though. She'd make a point of filling me in on the lesson as soon as she arrived home.

After glancing at the wall clock, she spun toward the front door. As she stepped onto the porch, she called out, "I'll probably stay and socialize after we're finished." I knew that. My mother loved to chat. I'd already counted on an hour study, approximately thirty-minute fellowship time, and twenty-minute drive time. And had chosen a movie to fit the time-slot.

As the dust settled from my mother's whirlwind trip through the house, I popped a bowl of popcorn, grabbed a blanket, and made myself comfortable on the couch. After discovering the remote under a magazine, I flipped through the streaming channels until I came to my chosen flick. A vintage thriller. Not one of those hair-raising, spine-tingling movies that scare you to death so you can't sleep. But a low-budget, simple entertainment flick. I tend to be impressionable, so choose plots that won't show up in my nightmares.

I'd finished half the popcorn and a can of cola when startled by a thumping in the vicinity of the front porch. I checked my watch and paused the movie, thinking it odd that Mom had come home early, but I didn't want to miss any plot twists while she filled me in about the Bible lesson. Even cheap old movies warranted my full attention. I waited. When she failed to materialize, I flipped the go button.

After a few minutes, I hit the pause button again, having heard more noises outside. From the comfort of the couch I called. "Hello?" No answer. "Mom?"

Then I heard a sound that sent chills up my spine. A howling. Not exactly the wailing Willow had described. I wouldn't have called it unearthly, but combined with the other unexplained noises, it set my nerves on edge.

I grabbed my cell phone from my handbag and tiptoed to the window, cautiously shifting the curtain to one side. I opened it just enough to peek out. Call me paranoid, but bumps-in-the-night send my imagination spinning. And the howling wasn't helping. I pressed my face close to the window. The yard was dark so I slid my hand to the light switch and flipped on the porch light. I stared intently, barely breathing, expecting the trespasser to be revealed at any moment. Why hadn't I replaced the bulb weeks ago when I'd noticed it had dimmed? In the poor available light, I detected movement through the bushes.

With my imagination in full spin, I saw creatures everywhere. That's when a dark figure emerged from the shadows and moved through the corner of the yard, then into the shrubbery at the side. This wasn't imaginary. I gulped a breath and stifled a scream. My heart thumping.

I'm a grown woman. This couldn't be Bigfoot. They were not real. It was obviously only a thief… or an ax murderer. Whoever it might be, I didn't want to face it alone. Where would I find help, should this intruder attempt a break-in? I quickly discounted most of the neighbors. They were all old or not physically up to the task of rescuing me. I scrolled through the contacts on my phone, searching for a close neighbor who was under the age of, maybe, seventy. As I scrolled, the phone rang in my hand causing me to scream and fling it into the air. Crouching to the floor to collect the still ringing phone, swiped to answer. My greeting came out in the squeaky little voice that is all I can manage when I'm scared. The caller was my friend, Clair. "Hi. Just called to see how your day went. What's wrong with your voice?"

I hissed. "I'm so glad you called. There's a prowler in the yard and I don't know what to do. It's so dark out there, I can't tell who it is. Or what it is."

"Probably just kids."

"I don't think so."

"Maybe one of your neighbors is out and about?"

"They're all old and it's past their bedtime. Besides, they wouldn't be skulking around in the dark without letting me know what they were up to."

"Okay, then you better call the police."

"Do you think I should?" I paused to consider the move. "It's probably nothing. And they'll laugh at me. In this news-poor town, I'll be on the front page. That would be embarrassing. My mother will have a fit if she comes home and the police are here for no reason."

"Just trying to help you, here. Umm. Get the handgun from the cupboard."

"The gun? Unh-unh. Nope. I hate guns." It had been a surprise when my mother disclosed her shady past. I could have passed out when she'd admitted there had been guns stashed in the house since before I was born.

"Girlfriend, you should learn to shoot."

"No way. You know me. Would you really trust me with a gun?"

"I see your point."

I inhaled a deep breath and got off the floor. "I can't stand here and do nothing. I'm going out on the porch and find out what's going on."

Clair raised her voice. "No. Wait. Take something

as a weapon."

"Good idea. But what?" I spun around to search. "I'll find something." Our old umbrella stood in the back corner of the hall closet. I pulled it out, weighing it in my hand. Sturdy, not one of those flimsy cheap things you buy on the spur of the moment when you weren't expecting rain. "Found something. I'm ready to go."

"Okay, but leave your phone on and carry it with you. I'll be able to hear what's going on."

"Great idea." I slid my cell phone into the pocket of my jeans and crept up to the window for another peek. The bushes were still moving. Could it be the monster that terrorized Willow? I whispered so Clair couldn't hear. "Lord, I'm sorry I laughed at Willow's story." If not Bigfoot, maybe a bear? Ax murderer? I took a deep breath and steeled myself to confront the intruder—man or beast.

"I can do this." I announced to the empty house—and Clair. "I am strong." Umbrella in hand and my friend on the phone, I yanked the door open and took two steps onto the porch. I shouted. "Who's out there?" There was no answer. It's no wonder, I sounded like a little girl. I deepened my voice and shouted again. "I have a gun and I'll use it. I can see you in the shrubbery. Come out and show yourself."

I detected movement in the bushes and backed up against the doorframe raising my umbrella. The dark figure had stepped closer into the dim light shining from the porch. I managed to see that it was a man. He appeared not very tall and sort of roundish. He was bent over and there was the sound of wheezing as he sucked in breath.

"Who's there?"

"Just a sec. Catching my breath." He held up his left hand to show a leash attached to a little wiggly white dog.

The man straightened and puffed. "I'm sorry to bother you, Ms. Cassell. It's me, George Trainor. I've been out here trying to catch my dog. He chased a rabbit into the landscaping. Sorry if his barking bothered you. I've got him now."

George motioned toward my umbrella, raised both hands, and laughed. "Please don't shoot. What caliber is that umbrella, anyway?"

"Very funny. I think you're safe."

"I apologize again for the commotion. This is Riley." The dog wagged his tail and barked at me. "I got him from a rescue last week. He's a Westie and they warned me his breed loves to dig. I didn't fully understand. I figured my fenced-in yard would do the trick, but the scamp has learned how to dig his way out. I fill in the holes and it slows him down for a while but he's a persistent little thing. This is the second time today that I've had to chase him."

"We'll be getting home. Good evening." George put up a hand to wave and the two of them faded into the darkness of the street.

I'd turned to go inside when I heard snickering from my pocket. Remembering Clair, I pulled out my cell phone and put it to my ear hearing hiccups of laughter. "I'm glad you were entertained by my traumatic experience."

Clair managed to catch her breath. "Thank goodness you had your umbrella."

"Ha. Ha. At least I didn't call the police. And I

won't be featured in the morning news." I would, I could tell, be putting up with Clair's ribbing for a while.

Clair had squelched her giggles. "I'm sorry I laughed at you. I'm sure it was a scary thing being home alone."

I'd predicted Willow was apt to cause hysteria. But didn't really think it would be me. I wondered if Mr. Trainor had been chasing Riley in Willow's neighborhood. That would explain the intruders in her property. And maybe calm her fears. Best not to say anything and hope she'd already forgotten about it. Besides that, I'd have to admit to brandishing an umbrella at my own imaginary monster.

Chapter Three

My job is almost always easy and pleasant. It may be tedious but I don't mind being the bookkeeper for this little business. I like it. I do. Mostly. I'm not a complainer. I pride myself on my cheerful attitude. But someone had messed up. Their one mistake had added hours to my work day. I'd struggled through accounts most of the morning, trying to figure out what someone had forgotten to enter in the daily reports. I suspected Mr. Bennett. Who else would it be? There were only the two of us in the hardware store. Well, there was Jimmy Conklin who did sweeping and dusting on weekends. But he knew better than to touch the cash register.

Anyway, I'd been searching for the error long enough for my eyes to cross. A shrill ping from my cellphone rescued me from an increasing desire to cuss. The text from my friend Clair read 'Meet me at The Caffeinated Cup?'

I shot a quick reply and offered up a grateful prayer to God who always knew when I'd had enough. Conversation about anything other than flat head nails promised to be welcome relief on this day.

I gathered my bag and jacket, informed Mr.

Bennett of my intention, and trotted out the door before anything else required my attention.

The sign on the door—Welcome Home—broadcast the coffee shop's intention that everyone should feel at home. Walls painted in various shades from rich coffee brown to caramel to cream. Chairs upholstered for comfort. All created an atmosphere inviting me to live there. As always, the warm aroma of freshly ground coffee enveloped me as I stepped through the door. Clair waved from her favorite seat, next to the window. I stopped at the counter to collect a latte and slid into a chair across from her.

I eyed the golden scone resting on a crystal plate next to her coffee. "Orange cranberry?"

Clair nodded. "Fresh and still warm."

"Can't resist that." I got up and returned to the counter to get one of my own. By the time I'd returned to the table I'd taken my first bite and moaned my joy. "Yum. This is wonderful. But I find it hard to believe my health-food freak friend is eating anything this sweet in the middle of the day."

Clair raised her eyebrows at me and gave me a quirky half-smile. "I have permission. My natural food gurus insist it's important to treat yourself once in a while so you don't resort to binging on sugar." She broke off a piece of scone and popped it into her mouth. "How's your day?"

"Hmm. You know. Same as every day." I felt the first threads of complaint beginning, so took a large bite of scone and stared out the window. I hate it when someone feels the need to spoil the mood. I wasn't going to be one of those people.

Clair picked up a crumb from her plate. "This is

my favorite place to be. If I could move Michael in here, life would be perfect."

"Do you think they have a spare room in the back?" Clair simply grinned. Her husband, Michael, had the prettiest blue eyes, loved all animals and most people.

My friend took a slow slurp of her coffee and smiled. "The scent of fresh ground coffee, delicious food, good friends, and a place to watch the world go by outside."

Clair tapped the window with a well-manicured index finger. "Look. There's Willow Ottenweller. She lives in that old Victorian home beside Bird Song Park. It must be the oldest structure in town. It's too bad she doesn't update it. Probably would cost a fortune, though."

I watched as Willow struggled to cross the street, and got up to slide my chair back. "That bag she's carrying is almost as big as she is. I'll see if I can do anything for her." As I started to make my way to the door with plans to help, Willow steadied the huge bag of dog food and marched on. I settled back into my chair. "Guess she's okay. I didn't know she had a dog. I've never seen it at the park."

Clair lifted her shoulders. "Maybe she's getting one." She squinted out the window. "A big one."

"Speaking of Willow Ottenweller, she livened things up at Bennett's the other day. I'm a little worried about her. She stormed in, and you wouldn't believe the crazy tale she told." I leaned on the table and spent a few minutes filling Clair in on Willow's monster story.

"Then, I stopped at the Market on the way home. And would you believe Willow had already been there spreading the nonsense? My neighbor, Linda, works there as a checker. And she fell for the fairy tale. If Willow keeps it up, someone is going to have her committed. She's such a sweet old lady, I'd hate for that to happen."

Clair shifted her cup and watched her coffee swirl. "Unless it's true."

"What? That Willow is bonkers?"

"No. That the Crosley Monster was in her back yard."

Please Lord, don't let me explode. I replied to my friend as sweetly as I could. "They don't exist. If they did, we would hear of a lot more sightings."

"The forests over near Crosley have miles of deep undergrowth. Plenty of room for animals, or whatever, to live and to hide. The fact that they've stayed out of sight most of the time doesn't mean the creatures aren't living there." Clair paused for a moment. "And I wish they weren't called monsters. That makes everyone afraid of them."

I took a deep cleansing breath. "Please tell me you don't really believe that stuff."

Clair shrugged and took another sip of coffee. She remained silent.

I couldn't believe I was arguing about the existence of Bigfoot with one of the few sane people I knew. "I agree there have been strange sightings in the forest. But it's easy to imagine shapes and shadows in thick woods. And why would there be one in Twin Fawn?"

"Maybe he decided to explore and traveled at night." She paused. "Just throwing ideas out there. That park has become popular lately. What if there were so many people hiking in the woods that the creatures have been forced to venture out? Probably looking for a better place to live."

"And nobody spotted an eight-foot-tall hairy creature walking from Crosley, Indiana to Twin Fawn. And, by the way, Willow said the monster was blond."

She lifted a shoulder. "It could happen."

I stared at my friend, praying for a punch-line. "Unbelievable. You of all people, believing in a Bigfoot monster?"

"Listen girl. In my years of selling houses, I've heard all kinds of strange stories. And I've seen some weird stuff, too."

She leaned across the table and whispered. "I sold a haunted house, once. A real haunted house. I saw floating shadows, felt cold spots, and heard things. Scared me so much that when I took prospective buyers for a showing, I wouldn't even go inside. I made an excuse for staying out and let them tour it alone."

I gulped my coffee. "Just to be clear, you said you sold someone an actual haunted house?"

"Sure did. The poor seller needed to unload it. If I told the buyers what I believed, they would have thought I was crazy. And I'd have lost a sale." She leaned back in her chair. "You'll find people who deny it, but there's a lot more going on in this world than what we can explain."

Ella, the waitress, came to wipe off the table next to us. She glanced up at the counter, then leaned toward us. "Have you heard? Keep your pets inside if you don't want them to be eaten. The Crosley Monster is in Twin Fawn. Willow Ottenweller was in this morning. She saw it in her yard a couple nights ago. She said it was ten feet tall and screamed like a banshee."

Having offered her caution, Ella straightened and scurried away.

I shook my head. "Lord, help us. The gossip train is working overtime and adding to the tale as it goes along. That isn't even the story Willow told. Her bad dream is bound to end up causing mass hysteria."

Clair waved her hand at me. "It'll be over in a week. The creature will probably be on his way home anytime. Especially if he has a family. It would be too dangerous here in Twin Fawn. Too many people. Maybe he's already left town."

I leaned on my elbows and slurped my latte. "Gosh. Maybe I'm the one having the nightmare."

Chapter Four

Once again, I wandered to the Caffeinated Cup after an early finish at work. As I said, it's a daily habit. With any luck Clair would be joining me. After my text, she reminded me of an open-house in progress, but promised to drop by later.

I pushed open the front door and immediately pulled in a deep breath, rewarded with the lovely aroma of the shop's signature coffee. The lunch rush had cleared out and the after-work crowd had yet to arrive, so there was no line at the counter. In fact, I happily had the whole place to myself. I stepped up to the counter and gave Ella my order.

While she filled a cup, I glanced around. "You've changed things a bit." The coffee shop now displayed an assortment of lush green plants. Containers dangled in macrame hangers from the front window and a few pots sat on the larger tables.

The proprietress grinned. "Yeah. Since the weather is changing outside, we thought we'd add some fresh greenery to get us through the winter."

Ella's attention was diverted when another customer lumbered in with a hand propped on his lower back. I dipped my head and sneaked to a table to avoid eye contact. Oscar White had lived in Twin Fawn for over eighty years. That was my guess. I had no idea of his age, but I knew he was old and given to lengthy conversations. Not really conversations, more narrations, since they were all one-sided. His side. There weren't many Twin Fawn residents that I didn't like, and it wasn't that I disliked Oscar, but I couldn't say I enjoyed his company.

His voice carried as he had a captive audience with Ella. "You've heard, I suppose, that the town council wants to buy Willow Ottenweller's house to tear it down. They say they want to enlarge Bird Song Park."

Ella grabbed a rag and wiped the countertop. "Uh huh. I heard that."

"You'll agree with me that it isn't right that the town tears it down without her consent. Government's getting out of control." He paused almost long enough to wait for a reply, but not quite. "I've got an idea. That house is the oldest structure in Twin Fawn. And as such, it should be declared a historical landmark. You could get a petition together. Put it here beside the cash register and present it to all your customers. Wouldn't take long to get enough signatures. That would stop the council in their tracks."

Ella continued scrubbing the counter harder and faster. I thought she might take the glossy finish off before Mr. White finished with her. "Oscar. I can't be seen to take sides. It would be bad for business. A lot of patrons of The Caffeinated Cup are in favor of a bigger park. As a matter of fact, I'm for it, too." She stopped cleaning to look him in the eye. "Are you here for coffee?"

Oscar gave a grunt. "Yes."

Ella poured his coffee into a to-go cup and set it in front of him.

"Can't believe you'd agree to it. That's a big disappointment. Tell you what. I'll construct the petition and drop it off to you. Leave it here on the counter. You'll find there's support for it." Oscar laid down his payment, said something about his back acting up, and trudged out. Ella glared at him as he left, then threw the rag into the sink.

Having the coffee shop to myself once more, I took a deep breath, inhaling the essence of the thriving plants mingled with the fresh ground coffee. After her conflict with Oscar, I figured Ella could use some encouragement. "I love your coffee shop. I could stay here and happily drink coffee all day." I'm not sure even the sociable owner, Ella, would agree to that. "How long would you put up with me before charging me with loitering?" And, although I loved the coffee, The Caffeinated Cup's brew barely fit my budget at one five-dollar cup a day. I had taught myself to sip slow to make it last.

Ella smiled and restacked her stash of to-go cups.

The shop was quiet except for some soft meditative music. I felt exceptionally blessed as I carried my second cup—a free refill—to the table by the window. The new flower pot hanging nearby contained a lovely vine with leaves of green and purple stripes.

I twisted toward the counter and attracted Ella's attention. "This vine is beautiful. What is it?"

She smiled. "It's Tradescantia Zebrina."

"Um, okay. What would a lay person call it?"

"It has a common name, but my aunt, who was

kind enough to donate these plants, is a master gardener. She insists we only use their true names. She's also a retired teacher and wants everyone to learn to look them up."

After she spelled it for me, I tapped my phone to begin the search for the plant.

I hadn't gotten very far when the shop door swooped open, pushed by two fast moving customers. Being acquainted with them, I did the neighborly thing and put up a hand to hail a greeting. It only took a moment to get the message. They were in no mood for friendly banter. I closed my mouth and directed my attention to the plant.

The crackly little voice of Willow Ottenweller echoed through the shop. "How many times do I have to tell you? I'm not selling my house!" She pointed toward the counter. "Just get me a plain coffee." Willow's son, Johnny, dutifully collected the coffees and delivered them to a table at the back of the room where Willow waited.

Johnny's voice seemed deliberately controlled. Unfortunately, the words came out stilted as if meant for a feeble mind. "The town council is offering you a fair price. Especially since you haven't put any money into that place for years. No updates. The few repairs we've done ourselves. Think of what you could do with the cash from the sale."

Willow's words picked up steam. "I don't care what the town council wants to do, I won't leave that house until they deliver my body to the mortician. It's my home. I was born there. Your father and I set up housekeeping in it after we got married. You lived there from the time you were two days old. What good is money without my home?"

 Willow paused to slurp coffee and take a breath. "I don't understand why you want to give it away. You were raised in that house. Your little bare feet tracked through every room. You lived in that house your entire life until you went to college and got married. So many memories."

 "First of all, Mom, I'm not asking you to give it away or be homeless. With the money from the sale, you can secure a nice place. Maybe at Clairmont Retirement Community. There would be people close by if you needed anything. No lawn mowing, no upkeep on the house. Just enjoy yourself."

 I actively listened to their conversation. Didn't think it would be called eavesdropping when their words were broadcast throughout the coffee shop.

 Johnny began to sound a bit frustrated. He took a deep breath. "Mom. You're not getting any younger. And the house is aging faster than you are. There's something that needs fixing every time I come to town. Face it. The old thing is falling apart."

 Willow gasped. "My home is not falling apart. Every house needs minor repairs, periodically. If you can't be bothered to help your mother, I can do them myself."

 Johnny tried another tactic. "You're just being stubborn. Don't tell me you have emotional bonds to the house because of Dad. I sure don't. He was self-centered and mean. You act as if he died. He didn't, he deserted us when I was, what, twelve or thirteen? He's out there somewhere. You were left to handle everything on your own. It's time you had something for yourself."

Willow had lost some of her bluster, but she snapped. "Don't talk about your father like that."

"You've always stuck up for him. Why do you do that? We haven't even heard from him since he left. Unless you have and you neglected to inform me. Have you?"

"No." Willow stared at the table. I thought she might be fighting back tears. "I don't want to talk about him. He's still your father. You need to respect that."

Johnny let out a breath. "Okay. I'll respect your wishes. But back to the point. I don't like the idea of you being alone in that big place. It's a tinderbox. Could catch on fire."

"I have a fire extinguisher."

"What if something happened to you? You might fall and break a bone or get sick. I live four hours away and it would take me forever to get here after I managed to get off work."

"I have friends in Twin Fawn who check on me more than you do."

Johnny blustered. "I know you have friends, Mom. But if you fell and couldn't get up, you might be on the floor all night and probably half the next day. In an apartment, people are closer and would hear you if you called out. I really think it is the best solution."

I admired the little woman's fighting spirit. Listening to her defend herself broke my heart. I felt an urge to get out of my chair and fight for her. Thankfully, good sense told me not to butt in. This argument was between a mother and her son.

I stole a glance in their direction. Willow had turned her chair so that she faced away from Johnny. "You aren't thinking right." She guzzled her coffee and

Johnny slumped in his seat. It looked as though they had exhausted their arguments.

Willow pushed up from her chair and plunked her empty cup on the table. Johnny scooped it up and took it, with his, to the counter. While there he whispered an apology to Ella. She gave him a sympathetic smile and a pat on the hand.

Clair arrived at the Caffeinated Cup a minute later and held the door as Willow stomped out, her son trailing after her. Willow's elderly little legs carried her at a surprising pace, leaving Johnny to jog in order to catch up.

Clair joined me and motioned toward the unhappy pair hustling down the street together, but not speaking to one another. "What went on with Willow Ottenweller and that man?"

"That was her son, Johnny. You should have heard them argue about selling her house. He's all for unloading it. Said he's worried about her living alone and trying to take care of everything. I understand his point of view but I feel sorry for her. She's against the sale. It isn't fair that she should be forced out. I wish they could find a better solution." I took a breath and thought about what Willow had said about older women not being listened to.

"Here's something I learned from their… discussion." Clair twisted toward me expectantly. "Did you know her husband left them when Johnny was a teen? I've lived here all my life and hadn't heard that bit of gossip. I knew she'd been single for a long time but thought she was widowed. Johnny has no fond memories of his father. I guess the guy was difficult to live with and then up and disappeared."

Clair lifted her shoulders. "I didn't know that. But the house hasn't been listed for sale, so I wouldn't have heard its history or any gossip connected to it."

She paused to concentrate on her coffee. "Any home is a lot for one person, particularly an elderly woman. That place is a monstrosity. Too big and too old. I wonder how she heats it. All the windows look like they'd be drafty. I doubt that it is sufficiently insulated."

I pondered the situation, still trying to find logical support for Willow's side. "You're right, of course. Willow would be safer somewhere else and would likely discover that she really enjoyed a smaller, more updated, place. But I think it should be her choice."

I stopped. Another thought had popped into my head. "Wait. I hadn't even considered her weird rantings about Bigfoot. I wonder if she's developing dementia."

Clair was quiet and narrowed her eyes, so I continued. "Do you still think that story about Bigfoot might be true? You believe she really saw some kind of Sasquatch monster?"

Clair eyed me. "We call it the Crosley Monster. Lots of people have seen it, but haven't admitted it. Who wants to be labeled as crazy? I think Willow's mind is fine. In any event, she may be getting too old to care for that house alone."

"Oh, I forgot. You sold a haunted house." I would drop the imaginary monster discussion. We sat quietly and sipped our coffee.

After a while, I began to wonder. "Why do you think Willow is so intent on keeping her house? From what Johnny said, there weren't good memories. He certainly didn't have kind words for his father. And Willow didn't bother to defend her husband. Just told her son he needed to be respectful."

Clair drained the last dregs of coffee and set the mug on the table. "So, her husband deserted her and their boy. And he just disappeared? It must have been a struggle to keep things going. If it had been me, I'd have sold the house a long time ago to cut expenses."

"Me too." I finished my coffee. We returned our mugs to Ella, tossed our napkins, and waved goodbye.

~~~

Since my mother moved in with me, it had become my habit to make my presence known by calling 'I'm home' as soon as I walked in the door. She did the same. We were both still jumpy after a mad man had attempted to break in. He'd been carted off to prison long ago, but neither my mother nor I appreciated being surprised by visitors.

She called "hello" from the living room and met me in the hallway. She wore the same bright smile she'd worn every day since she quit the library. It was either the change of career or the arrival of Jack Reed in Twin Fawn. I had to admit the retired police officer, turned private detective, was almost as attractive as his son, Garrett. While Garrett sported thick dark brown hair that set off hazel eyes, blue-eyed Jack's hair had turned a striking silver. Jack and my mother had hit it off right away when he showed up at our door. The only problem I saw in their relationship was that she'd had business cards printed, Kat Cassell, assistant private investigator. Her name was Katherine, for goodness sake. And does anyone want to see their mother snooping into the private lives of strangers? Or chasing bad guys? There aren't many strangers in Twin Fawn, so snooping into the lives of acquaintances would prove even more awkward.

Anticipation bubbled in my mother's voice. "I'm on my way to meet Jack. We have a stakeout tonight."

"Please. No one wants to imagine their mother sitting in a car, taking photos of someone's illicit affair. Does Jack have a camera with one of those long-range lenses? Do you drink coffee and eat cookies while you wait for something incriminating to show up in the window? Oh, you don't sneak through the bushes on foot, do you?"

She laughed. I liked that. This happened a lot more often since Jack came into the picture. "This case isn't about anyone's adulterous affair. Nothing so romantic. But I can't talk about it. Jack signed a non-disclosure agreement."

I shook my head. "Better if I don't know. I prefer thinking of you at the library, sorting books. But I have a question before you go."

She planted her feet in front of me and gazed at me with wide eyes. "What would you like to know?"

"I saw Willow Ottenweller at the Caffeinated Cup having an argument with her son. What happened to her husband? I heard, today for the first time, that he deserted the family. And that he wasn't a nice guy. With Twin Fawn's gossip train, I can't believe I'd never heard about it."

My mother sighed. "Harley Ottenweller. Hadn't thought about him in ages. I don't know what happened to him. I don't think anyone does. At least no one ever said anything to me. I'd see him in town occasionally, and one day he just wasn't around anymore. He was not likeable. Egotistical, thought only of himself. I guess you'd say he had an exaggerated sense of self-importance. He would never lend a hand if someone was in need, least of all his own family."

Her smile had vanished as my mother thought back in time. "That man wasn't a nice person, so no one missed him enough to ask where he went. We all kept our thoughts to ourselves out of respect for Willow. We felt sorry for her and didn't want to cause her any more pain. I think Johnny was only about thirteen or so. We all gathered around them with smiles on our faces and pretended nothing had happened."

"You never wondered?"

"Of course, I thought about it occasionally. But from what I knew of his character, I figured Willow and Johnny, and all of us, were better off without him."

"And nobody ever looked for him?"

"No. It sounds strange to say it now but there was no reason to. Absolutely no chance of getting financial support for Willow and Johnny."

Mom pulled on a sweater and stepped onto the porch. "If Harley had come back, he'd have—been nothing but dead weight."

Chapter Five

My boss pulled on his well-worn overcoat, threadbare in places and looking like he might have been wearing it for the last twenty years. I couldn't imagine him in anything else as he stood at the door of Bennett's Hardware. "I won't be long Libby. I'll just catch up on a few errands. With this cold snap, I doubt you'll have many customers for the rest of the afternoon."

Mr. Bennett stepped out into the frosty air. Running errands was as good an excuse as any. I suspected he simply wanted to get out of the store. A widower for the past ten years, the man didn't seem to have much of a social life. As far as I knew, his days consisted of managing Bennett's Hardware and going home to watch television. And maybe church once or twice a week. What did men his age do for fun? There was no girlfriend in the picture. At one time, I was sure Mr. Bennett and my mother would be a good match. My mistake. A new side of Mom's personality had blossomed when Jack Reed arrived in town. Her bursts of energy would wear Mr. Bennett out in no time.

The time clicked by with few customers venturing in. Mr. Bennett was right about the weather keeping people at home. This was my kind of work schedule. Ringing up a few orders for regular customers produced little stress. With the store completely empty, I grabbed the feather duster to dab at some of the displays. At least, while dusting, I appeared to be productive—working to earn my weekly wage. Only a light layer of dust lined the shelves. Jimmy Conklin did a good job of cleaning on weekends.

While at the back of the store, working on some of the easily overlooked shelving, I was startled when the front door swung open. The store front, bright and sunny all morning, dimmed as if someone had switched off the sun. The feather duster slipped from my hand and I gulped air at first sight of the of a huge, sort of furry-looking creature silhouetted in the doorway. I squinted and worked on calming my breathing, trying to figure out what had happened to the light. The massive visitor stood very tall. He took two slow steps and landed in a pool of light streaming in from the side window. "Oh." I felt my heartbeat slow, then relax. The large shadowy creature turned out to be Maximus Bailey, a local farmer and easily the largest man in town. The big man owned land a few miles north of town and spent long days caring for it. His size could be intimidating, but in my experience, he'd always been humble and kind. He continued his slow gate down the aisle toward me. I almost laughed out loud when I focused on the over-sized coat he wore. The furry jacket nearly doubled his apparent girth.

"Good afternoon, Maximus. It's good to see you."

He raised a few fingers in a wave. "Afternoon."

"Love the jacket. I bet it keeps you toasty in this weather."

He smiled a little half-grin and patted his coat. "Isn't it something? My sister gave it to me. She called it a sherpa. Said she saw it and thought of me. Who else could wear a coat this size? It'll keep me warm on the farm."

Maximus hesitated at a display of garbage cans along the wall. He picked one up, using only his fingertips. It was one of our heavy-duty cans. Even the man's fingers were strong. After inspecting the can he replaced it but gathered a few other articles before stopping at the cash register. The man blocked most of the light that should have been streaming in, and I stood in his shadow while ringing up his purchase.

I shoved his supplies into a brown paper bag and handed it to him. "Have a good day, Maximus."

He nodded and gave a little wave.

Maximus lumbered from the store, while another customer wedged her way past him at the door. I'd have to say this woman was the opposite of Maximus, in every way. Lovey Henderson, petite and innocent—apparently—stood less than five foot tall. She wore high heels and a stylish baby blue coat that, I had to admit, complimented her long pale blonde hair. Although I doubted it kept her warm.

As Maximus plodded down the sidewalk, she stretched her neck to stare after him, mouth open. "I think we've found the Crosley Monster." Then she giggled and turned on her heel to scan the aisles.

It is our practice at Bennett's Hardware to always be nice to customers, but pleasant banter with her held little interest for me. And never at the expense of someone else. Lovey and I had never been friends. Her snobbish attitude being a big part of the gulf between us.

"Can I help you find something?" I thought she might be lost since I'd never seen her in the hardware store. Lovey managed a local dress shop, owned by her parents. I doubted she had ever held a hammer or even knew how one would be used.

Lovey shrugged and strolled through the sales room. "Daddy sent me after one of those hooky things. He wants to stick it to the underside of a shelf and hang keys on it."

It took me a few minutes to decipher her meaning, but finally showed her the screw-in wall hooks. I wanted to laugh at her explanation but couldn't because I didn't know what they were called, either.

She chose a couple hooks and brought them to the register. "Growing your hair out?" She inspected my hair while I stood speechless.

I managed to mumble, "No."

Lovey paid no attention. "Isn't it maddening trying to get through that awkward in-between stage? Don't you worry, eventually it will get some shape to it. Hair color would probably brighten it up. Definitely would give you more body and add a little life to it. But you've never cared for that sort of thing, have you?"

I grabbed a sack and stuffed her hooks into it tearing the bottom of the bag. "Crap." I grabbed another, praying she would leave the store before I spoke my mind.

Lovey had stepped toward the window and glanced out, but not in preparation to exit. "That creature. Do you think it's the one scaring old Mrs. Ottenweller?"

Not sure I heard her right. "What creature?" I paused to stare at her. "Do you mean Maximus?"

"Of course. I'm not one to believe in scary tales, but if that isn't a Bigfoot, it's a close relative."

She noticed I didn't join her in unkind chatter and flipped her long hair over a shoulder. "I'm not being catty. Don't you think he's weird? Everyone says so."

I kept my voice calm. "No. I don't think he is weird. He seems nice enough to me."

"I would never have occasion to talk to him but other people say you can't get a good conversation out of him. I've only seen him around town. Look how big he is." She paused while she closed the top button of her coat. "Probably a cross-breed."

I stood stunned and speechless, before finding words. "He's quiet, but I think that's because he's shy."

"He might be dangerous. I'm not afraid, of course. If I need to go out at night, I ask Garrett to go with me." She grinned. "He's so strong, not even the Crosley Monster would dare approach me. I always feel safe with Garrett."

I bit my tongue. Hurt like crazy but kept me from striking out. I should have known she would fit that reference into the conversation. She never missed a chance to mention her relationship with Garrett Reed. I'd known both of them since high school. Lovey, cheerleader and the most popular girl in school. Garrett the most handsome boy—man—in town. I'd had a crush on him since school, but we were just friends. Just friends. Our relationship had never grown into more and wouldn't as long as Lovey was in the picture. They'd started dating after her divorce from the former football hero a couple years back.

She gasped. "Oops. I almost forgot to pay you. Daddy gave me his card."

I'd almost forgotten to collect. Too intent on keeping my mouth shut.

Lovey pulled the credit card from her sparkly little blue handbag—geez, it matched her coat—and handed it to me.

While I ran it through the machine, she motioned toward the street, where Maximus had gone. "Just wait. They'll find it's him roaming around at night. His clothes are always dirty. Haven't you noticed?"

"Um. He's a farmer." I struggled to find more words, but Lovey Henderson had taken her card and finally removed herself from the hardware store and from my presence. She hadn't changed since her days as high school beauty queen. I hated having to talk to her and I couldn't help feeling old and drab when she was around.

As soon as the door banged shut, I grabbed my handbag, pulled out my cell, and called Clair. "Do you think I should highlight my hair?"

"What? Who is this? Lib?"

I took a deep breath. "Yeah. Sorry. I was having a moment. Lovey Henderson just left the store. I'll be okay in a minute."

"Hold it together Libby. I don't think you need a highlight. Unless you want one. Your hair is fine. You don't even have any gray, do you?"

"I don't think so." I started to pull out my mirror from my handbag, but tossed it back in. "Forget it. I'm okay, now."

"Don't listen to Lovey Henderson. You have so much more going for you than she does."

"I know." I paused for a moment. "Do you really think so?"

"Yes! You have so many friends. People actually like you. They only put up with Lovey Henderson because she runs the only dress shop in town. Quit thinking about her."

"Yes, I will." I sighed with relief. "Thank you. I feel better."

"Clair, while I have you on the phone, Lovey said something that is making me think. She compared Maximus Bailey with the Crosley Monster. She said maybe he's the one skulking around and scaring Willow Ottenweller. Do you know who he is?"

"Sure. I've seen him in the veterinary clinic. That man is hard to miss. But why would Lovey say that?"

"I guess, because he's such a big guy. And when he came into the store today, he wore a sherpa coat. You know the furry kind? When he first walked in, Bigfoot is the first thing that entered my mind. But only for a minute, until he moved out of the shadows and I saw his face."

Clair laughed. "I agree Maximus probably resembles Bigfoot more than anyone else in town. But you know better and so does Lovey Henderson. It sounds as if she needed something to talk about. You know how she tends to pick on people."

"You're right. I don't know why I listened to her. Maximus is a bit socially awkward, but I can't imagine he would be wandering around Twin Fawn after dark."

In the next hour, I spent time up close to the mirror searching for gray hairs. Didn't find any, but considered calling my hairdresser about the highlights.

While waiting for Mr. Bennett to return from running his errands I did a lot of people watching and thinking about my mother's favorite quotation. 'You can't judge a book by its cover.' What else would it be? She'd served Twin Fawn as librarian for years. Lovey appeared beautiful until you got to know her. Maximus sometimes looked scary, but he was a gentle soul. Willow seemed like a crazy old lady. The jury was still out on that one.

And Willow's tale about the Crosley Monster? I knew it was a Bigfoot myth. But was it possible Willow saw something, or someone else that scared her?

Chapter Six

As soon as Mr. Bennett returned to the store, I cut my workday short. I didn't care about the freezing temperatures outside. I still felt the need to cool off. So, I parked my car at home and grabbed gloves and wool scarf before I set off for a walk.

The encounter with Lovey Henderson still haunted my thoughts, and chipped away at my self-esteem. I hoped a stroll through Bird Song Park would push her and her malicious comments out of my head. The park failed to live up to its name on this afternoon. No bird songs or warbles. No chirping or cooing. Most song birds were well on their way south for the winter.

I made it a point to go by Willow Ottenweller's house hoping to visit with her for a while. I preferred to chat with the kindly older woman who entertained a few unrealistic fears, rather than the snobbish younger woman who was anything but kind and seemed capable of leaving deep gouges in my subconscious.

I found Willow on her knees, in her side yard, gripping a hand trowel. As she busily chopped at the dirt around some obviously dead plants, she failed to notice my approach.

I called to her while still at a distance. "Good

afternoon, Willow." She continued to dig, likely so intent on her work that she didn't hear me. I kept walking closer and raised my voice. "Still working in your gardens, I see." Stating the obvious is not my best stab at a conversation starter. I tried again. "Isn't it too late in the year to do them any good?"

She pushed her wispy white hair from her face and glanced up at me. "Hello, Liberty. It's good to see you." She said this with a smile that I knew to be genuine. A far cry from that of Lovey Henderson. "Plants need tending all year round, as long as the ground isn't frozen solid. Just like we need God's tending in the good times and the bad." She lifted a bundle of what appeared to be sticks with dead roots. "I'm taking these to plant in the back yard. Should have been done earlier in the year, but they'll appreciate it now."

"Can I help you?" This was one of those questions you ask to be polite while secretly hoping for a negative response. I didn't love gardening in the best of weather.

"No thank you, Liberty. That's very kind of you, but they're my babies and accustomed to my hand. I wouldn't want them to rebel at a stranger poking around."

"I had no idea plants would know one gardener from another. And you're telling me plants can rebel?"

Willow stared deep into my eyes. "Sure. They are living creatures. Aren't we all subject to a few bad habits once in a while? Take roses for instance. You'll see I don't have any of those in my yard. They're very prickly, both physically and emotionally. Including them in the community would cause an outright revolt."

"Uh-huh."

"All the growing things on this property have a

deep heritage with me. None of my plants have ever had another home. They know me and they're fond of each other. It's like we're related." While I contemplated that revelation, she pushed herself up from the ground. "Come around to the side of the house and I'll show you the rest of the family. I'd introduce you, but most of my children have finished blooming and already sleeping for the winter."

I nodded to express understanding. "Huh."

As we walked, I scanned what at one time, were plots of blooms. "You really take care of them. Even now, in the cold weather, they are beautiful." This was probably an over-statement.

My attention was attracted to a small building in the side yard. "I've seen your gazebo from the park, but never up close." It had obviously been there for a few years. The aged wood had mellowed but still appeared sturdy and inviting. "It's charming. If I lived here, I wouldn't get any work done because I'd want to sit in it all the time." I'd taken a few steps toward the gazebo with the intention of doing just that when Willow stepped up.

She planted herself between me and the building, moving to guide me in another direction. "It is lovely isn't it." I spend a lot of time sitting here and listening to the birds, but today isn't a good day. As you can see, I've been working on the ground around it. Wouldn't want to disturb the new plantings."

"No. I wouldn't want to do that." I followed her guidance and thought it best not to ask her to explain how those dormant plantings could be disturbed when she'd already explained rebellious plants. There were many strange residents of Twin Fawn. Willow was proving to be one of the strangest. I had wondered at her belief in Bigfoot, but this impressed me as a new level of bizarre.

She walked beside me, leading me away, presenting a barrier between me and the gazebo. "Johnny built it for me when he was young. He did such a fine job. It's held up well ever since. All I do is dress it with a new coat of paint every couple of years."

Having assured herself I wouldn't touch her gazebo, Willow angled off to pluck dried blossoms from an almost bare hydrangea bush. I walked toward the back of the house to investigate some vines and nearly tripped over a large stainless steel dog bowl. "I didn't know you had a dog, Willow." This solved the mystery of the super-sized dog food bag I'd watched her lug past The Caffeinated Cup.

Willow twisted and took a step toward me. "Oh, I don't have a dog." She glanced toward her neighbor's house and whispered. "The neighbors don't need to hear us talking. They're not believers." She moved closer. "The food bowl is for the Crosley Monster. I told you about him." She lifted a shoulder and gazed at me. "Anyway, I figure he's hungry and if I feed him, he won't make such a mess of the garbage cans. It's working." She pointed at the dog bowl. "That was full last night. And this morning—empty."

I nodded. "Yep. The food's all gone. Have you seen him again?"

"Not recently, but as you can see, he's been here. I made sure to get a bowl big enough that he can take some food back to his family, if he has one." I thought Willow might think she fed Bigfoot, but likely had acquired a flock of very happy pet racoons.

The woman had begun to worry me. Dealing with mental illness had never been my strong suit. I figured my safest move would be a change of subject. Pivoting, I waved a hand at the gazebo. "Johnny must have been very talented to build that. Did his father teach him carpentry?"

Willow spun away from a nearby planting where she'd picked off more dead leaves. "His father wasn't around long enough to teach him anything. My boy built it, himself, right after Harley left. One day I woke up and the sweetheart was digging the foundation. He'd collected all the materials. Said he wanted to do something for me. The neighbor man came over and helped him some, but Johnny did the bulk of the work on his own."

She stood and faced me. "Johnny's a good boy. You've probably heard how he thinks I'd be better off in a retirement village, but he's wrong about that. I'm keeping this house. I'm sure he'll come around to my way of thinking, sooner or later."

While Willow crouched to the ground to continue gardening, I wandered around the yard gathering my courage, because I was about to intrude. This was something my mother had regularly reminded me not to do for as long as I could remember. I guess she may have relaxed her rule since she'd become an apprentice private detective. As I walked back to Willow's side, I called, "I know it's probably none of my business, but I heard your husband left the family. They say he was never heard from again. Is that true? Why did he leave?" I had no excuse. It was blatant nosiness.

"They got it right. He left, and I never talked to him again. He didn't tell me he was leaving, let alone why."

"Didn't you ever wonder where he went? Did you look for him? Didn't the police investigate? He should have been here to support you and your son."

Willow's head snapped up and I expected a rant letting me know I was correct about it not being my business. But she surprised me and answered sweetly. "Why would anyone investigate? There was no need. Johnny and I were happier without him. And as for support, I got a second job and we did just fine." She paused before returning to her garden work. "I had no reason to concern myself with him. He made the decision to leave, not me."

I left Willow to her gardening and on my way home, I spent the time contemplating the conversation with the sweet, if delusional woman. It couldn't have been easy dealing with the rejection of a spouse and raising a son, while working two jobs to make ends meet. Some people might have taken refuge in bitterness or alcohol. I might have fallen into depression.

Willow fed fairytale monsters and cared for personified plants. Was there harm in that? No one had stepped up to help her, years ago as a single mother. But someone should now. The question niggling me was how to help her? I'd been ready to defend her claim to her home, standing against her son. But was that the right move?

Chapter Seven

Mouthwatering aroma of roast chicken wafted in from the kitchen and set my stomach to growling. My mother had set the dinner table for three. I knew extra effort had gone into that meal because she'd invited Jack Reed to join us. This was no surprise. Since he'd returned to Twin Fawn and shown up at our door, Jack had become a frequent visitor, not only because my mother helped him in his detective business, but because their relationship had started to bloom. In the years since my father's fatal heart attack, she hadn't shown this much interest in any of the men in Twin Fawn. Not until Jack.

As the timer signaled the vegetables were cooked, our doorbell sounded in tandem. "I'll get it." I ran to open the door and found Clair on the porch, saying she'd stopped by for a chat.

My mother popped into the hallway from the kitchen. "Clair, dear. It's good to see you. You must stay and have dinner with us. I'll just go put out another plate."

Mom had already returned to the kitchen when Clair called. "No. I couldn't intrude."

I lowered my voice. "Please stay. Jack's here and I feel like a third-wheel, again."

Clair grinned. "It smells amazing in here, and Michael's working late. How can I refuse?" She raised her voice in answer to my mother. "I'd love to join you."

She skipped around me and strode to the table. "How can I help?"

I collected the vegetables from the kitchen. Jack carried in a platter with the chicken. Clair arranged the serving dishes on the table. When we were all in our seats, Mom smiled at Jack and took his hand. This signaled the joining of hands around the table while Jack prayed. "Heavenly Father, we are grateful for this food and ask for your blessing on it. Thank you for times like these, where family and friends can gather together and share a meal. In the holy name of Jesus. Amen."

"And amen." Mom passed the corn to Clair. "Did I hear you say that handsome husband of yours is working tonight? What's he doing for dinner?"

"He keeps the vet clinic open late once a week for people who can't get in during regular hours. He'll pick up a sandwich on his way home."

"We'll send a plate home with you. A sandwich won't do for the night." When my mother cooked, we had food for a crowd. She always managed to give the leftovers away, either sending it home with guests or sharing it with the neighbors.

Dishes were passed around the table while we spoke of the interesting parts of our day. Conversation was light. Not a lot of excitement going on in Twin Fawn, even with Jack's private investigation business.

My visit with Willow had been weighing on my mind, so when the conversation lagged, I jumped in. "I stopped by Willow Ottenweller's house today. We had a nice visit."

Mom passed the rolls to Jack. "How is Willow? I've been busy with my new endeavors and haven't seen her for a while."

I put down my fork, suddenly less interested in eating. "She seems fine, physically. But I'm worried about her mental state. She shared some strange thoughts with me."

Clair cut her eyes toward me. "Like what?"

I related Willow's ideas on her plants and their heritage. "Now that I've said it, I understand it seems silly and certainly not dangerous. But when combined with her Bigfoot sightings…"

I tore a roll in half. "Don't get me wrong. Willow has the right to believe what she wants. But if the wrong people hear the tales she told me, they may use it against her. There are those, like the town council, who would like to see her house torn down to enlarge the park."

Jack leaned toward me. "I hadn't heard of any Bigfoot sightings."

I related Willow's story of the Crosley Monster. Jack gave no indication of how he felt about the monster myth. He's a wise man and rarely gives opinions unless asked.

I glanced at Clair. "I know we disagree about Bigfoot, but Willow's taking it too far. She has a great big bowl outside her back door that she fills with dog food." I looked around at puzzled faces. "She doesn't own a dog. She's concerned the Crosley creature might be hungry, so she keeps the bowl filled for him—or it."

Mom shrugged and buttered a dinner role. "It's a bit odd but doesn't seem dangerous."

Clair, very aware of the importance of neighborhood relations from her work as a realtor, held her fork in the air. "Normally I'd say let her do what she wants, but leaving food out may cause problems. Both for the neighbors who believe in the Crosley Monster and those who don't. True believers might object to her inviting the thing to stay in the area. And those who don't believe will be afraid of her drawing other wild animals.

Jack grabbed a second roll. "Such as racoons, ground hogs, foxes. If she doesn't own a dog to eat the food and to chase those critters away, they'll be drawn to her yard. That can be a problem for home owners. She might be in for trouble. I suppose it'll depend on her neighbors. If they are gracious enough to ignore her eccentricities or not."

We were quiet as we finished eating. I regretted bringing it up. Was Willow really harming anyone by indulging her fantasies?

Soon, Jack encouraged us to get comfortable in the living room while he opened a bottle of wine he brought. "Katherine has these beautiful crystal wine glasses in the cupboard. We might as well put them to use. I'll pour."

While I held my glass for Jack to fill, I glanced at my mother. "Has Willow always been, you know, strange?"

My always kind and thoughtful mother took a moment to answer. "In the old days, Willow was quiet so I didn't get to know her well. I don't remember her having many friends. But we were all raising children and working, so we didn't have much time for socializing. I remember she seemed a little different. Never quite like the other mothers in town."

Mom gave a short laugh. "But who would want to be like everyone else? I tried that. It's hard work." She paused a moment and the smile went away. "I suppose Willow probably drifted farther away from us after her husband left."

Clair took a big gulp from her crystal wine glass. "What was the husband like?"

Mom leaned back and tipped her head toward Clair. "I remember Harley Ottenweller as not a nice man. He never seemed to be anyone I'd want to spend time with. And Liberty's father didn't want me around him."

This caught my attention. "I don't remember Dad ever telling you who you could be friends with."

"He didn't, except that once. I thought he must have had good reason. Come to think of it. I wondered at the time if your dad knew something about Harley that I didn't."

"Like what?"

Mom shrugged. "He never said."

Clair twisted toward Jack, who was looking drowsy sitting on the sofa with his feet propped up on the coffee table. "You were on the Twin Fawn police force, back then. Do you remember hearing anything about the man? It seems that if he had done anything unlawful, you would've known."

Jack shook his head. "No, I don't remember Harley Ottenweller. He must not have been in any trouble. You say he disappeared? As far as I know, no one reported him missing. You would think since she had a child, his wife would have tried to find him for child and spousal support. But nothing came through our office. Like Katherine said, no one missed him."

Clair put her empty wine glass on the coffee table. "That kind of thing makes me angry. I wish we could find Harley Ottenweller and sue him for back child support on Willow's behalf."

Jack paused for a moment and rubbed his chin. "That's an interesting thought. Johnny, of course, aged out of the child support need a long time ago. It seems that Willow could sue for back child support. But if she never filed in the first place, there wouldn't be any proof of what he owed."

I drained the last of my wine. "There isn't any point in looking into it. Willow made it clear she isn't interested in child support. In fact, she isn't interested in Harley at all. It looks like we're a lot more concerned than she is."

I sat quietly for a moment. "Even if it doesn't concern her, it concerns me. I'm curious to know where he went and what he's been doing all this time." Warming to the subject, I put up an index finger. "You know the stress of Willow's life—working so hard and raising her son—could have affected her mental state. It might be the cause of the emotional issues she's experiencing now."

Clair pointed at me. "You're right. If we found him, we could pour on the shame. Maybe threaten to make his past public wherever he lives now. Then we could squeeze some money out of him for Willow. Enough to update her house. Make it safer for her."

My mother raised her hand and waved at us.

"Woah, girls. If Willow isn't interested, and we know she isn't, it wouldn't be right to get involved. It isn't wise or kind to bring up old hurts. And right now, she has enough conflict with her son trying to take over. No matter how much money you think you could get out of Harley, it wouldn't be enough to fix all her problems."

I sulked for a moment. "Shoot. I hate it when you're the voice of reason."

After a moment, I rallied. "But I sure wish I knew where he went. Do you think you and Jack could at least check your internet sites and trace him? I wouldn't do anything with the information, but I'm curious to see if he's been hiding nearby."

My mother took a deep breath and gave up easier than I'd expected. She glanced at Jack and then nodded. "Okay. We'll look into it for you. But if we find him, I don't want you to try to get in touch with him. Don't do anything until we talk again. With him being such a jerk back then, he could be worse now. He might be dangerous."

My mother gave me an intense look. "Do you promise to stay away from him?"

I nodded but she glared at me until I spoke the words. "Okay. I promise." I made a little cross over my heart. But I still wanted to let Harley know what I thought of a man who wouldn't live up to his responsibilities.

Clair checked her watch and took her wine glass to the kitchen. "I'll get home just about the time Michael gets in."

My mother moved to the seat beside Jack. "Good night, Clair. Don't forget Michael's plate."

I walked my friend to the door and whispered,

"Mom's softening."

Clair grinned and winked. "Let me know what you find out."

While my mother was still in an agreeable mood, I offered to wash the dishes and clean the kitchen. As I expected, she and Jack volunteered to drive to his office and run some searches.

~~

I finished the kitchen and stretched out on the sofa to watch a movie. Later, I awoke to Mom's voice. I looked at the television screen. The movie was over, and I couldn't remember anything about it.

Mom plopped into the recliner. "Well, I'm surprised. Jack and I couldn't find a trace of Harley Ottenweller after June 19, 1993. He not only disappeared from Twin Fawn, but from all records. License branch, income taxes, everything."

"Jack even checked police records, banking records, everything you can imagine. He didn't tell me how and I didn't ask. He says it's best that I don't know everything. It looks to me like Harley must have changed his name."

"Why would he do that? I doubt Willow would've had the means to go after him for child support and spousal support, even if she'd wanted to. So, he didn't have to hide from her. Jack said he wasn't linked to any crime. So why?"

My mother maintained enthusiasm for the name change theory. "Maybe Harley had hoarded money and stashed it away. Enough to create a new identity or leave the country."

I stood and flipped off the television. "That might happen in the big cities. Did you forget this is Twin

Fawn? I never met the man but I think we're giving him far too much credit."

Mom laughed. "You're right. What was I thinking? He wouldn't have had the intelligence to change his identity." She leaned back and raised the leg rest. "Maybe he dropped dead somewhere and nobody ever found the body."

I laughed at the thought. "Uh-huh. You've been watching too much Unsolved Mystery. Even out in the farm land, someone would have found a body." I yawned and stretched. "We might never know. I'm going to bed."

~~

Somewhere around midnight I startled awake. A nightmare. In it, tiny Willow, cottony hair flying in the wind, chased her husband with an ax. I untangled myself from the sheets and pondered that possibility for a while. No. Not Willow, and not in Twin Fawn, Indiana. Willow wasn't the type to kill anything. And certainly not her husband. But, how did he disappear? And if Harley had been murdered, who would have done it? From my mystery watching, there seemed to be a problem with clean up after someone had been killed. People noticed things in a small town.

I couldn't sleep for the images running through my mind, so I got out of bed and went downstairs for a glass of orange juice. Sweet little Willow Ottenweller would never have chased anyone with an ax. And Johnny, at only thirteen or so when his father left had shown no signs of violence. He might have been old enough and strong enough to overpower a man, but he was no sociopath. I stood for a while in the dark kitchen, thinking on one glaring point.

SECRET MERCY

It probably wouldn't take much to hide a body if no one cared enough to look for it.

Chapter Eight

Snickering from the sales floor distracted me from my bookwork. While Mr. Bennett and I enjoyed good rapport, I couldn't say that laughter was a big part of our day. I recognized the giggles joining his. That melodic voice belonged to my friend, Clair. While tucked away, concentrating on checks and balances, I hadn't noticed her arrive. I pushed myself from the desk and peaked out my office door. Clair and Mr. Bennett stood with their heads together, still chuckling.

I summoned my fake stern voice. "What's going on out there?"

My boss let out another hearty laugh. "Clair's causing trouble."

"Is she telling jokes again? Taking you away from your duties?"

"You have to hear this, Libby." He glanced at Clair. "Let me tell her." He pivoted to face me and announced. "Clair has this friend who is completely bald. Lost all his hair years ago but he still carries around his old comb."

Pausing for effect and letting me stew waiting for the punch line, he gave me a Cheshire Cat smile. "He just can't part with it."

Both Mr. Bennett and my friend burst into peals of laughter again. I laughed, too, but mostly because of their joy, not the silly joke.

When the two had calmed themselves, Clair informed me that she'd already asked my boss if I could take the rest of the afternoon off.

"You asked if I could come out and play?"

She nodded. "And Mr. Bennett said yes."

My boss corrected her. "To be clear, I said that it's up to you. You know where you are in the books."

I could have jumped for joy, being more than ready to quit work for the day. Just waiting for a reason. "I'm at a perfect stopping point." A perk of living in a small town and being employed by a small business owner is the flexible work schedule. Almost any point is the perfect place to stop on any day.

I hustled back to my desk and closed the computer. After stuffing the day's receipts into a file, I slung my handbag over my shoulder and grabbed my jacket.

Clair waited at the front door. "You can take your car home and I'll pick you up there. Then we can decide where to go."

"Sounds good to me." I waved to Mr. Bennett and we left.

As we drove past Bird Song Park, I noticed a halo of wispy white hair hovering over a park bench. It could be none other than Willow Ottenweller. This surprised me because even though the sun was bright, the temperature was frigid. Yet she sat on the bench alone staring at her house. I wondered at it since she could have easily perched on her own front porch and been more comfortable. I had a feeling she needed a friend.

Clair followed close enough behind me that she recognized my hand signals directing her to pull over at the curb. We parked in adjoining spaces and walked together to the bench where the tiny woman sat. "What's up, Willow? Are you out here enjoying the sunshine?"

Her face brightened. "Liberty, just the girl I wanted to see. I needed to talk to someone and was just now praying you would show up. And I'm happy to see you, as well, Clair." She patted the bench. "You girls have a seat."

When we had settled on either side of her, she said. "Doesn't my house look nice there beside the park?"

We both nodded in agreement, although I was thinking it would be even nicer if the gutters were repaired and with a new coat of paint.

Willow continued. "I've been thinking that extra green space in the park would look even better. Can't you picture children playing over there? What a joy that would be."

I shifted in my seat to gaze at her, wondering what had happened to the stubborn woman who had recently vowed to fight to the death to save her home.

Willow smiled at me. "It took me a while but I've made the decision. I'm on my way to meet my boy Johnny and would be so grateful for your company. You two ladies will be my witnesses." She directed her attention to Clair. "It's perfect that you are here, also. I've heard you are in real estate. Just the subject I want to discuss with him."

She paused and shifted her gaze from Clair to me. "I'll need your support. If you're there with me, he won't talk me into changing my mind."

I put a hand on Willow's arm. "Of course, we'll go with you. But I'm confused. I thought selling the house is what Johnny wanted you to do. Why would he try to change your mind?"

Willow stood and smoothed the skirt of her dress. "You'll see."

The little woman took a deep breath and clenched her fists. "Let's go. Drive me up to the coffee shop."

While we trailed behind Willow like two little girls, Clair whispered to me. "What's going on?"

"I have no idea. Poor Willow. This is so at odds with her previous conviction, I'm afraid she's having a psychotic break."

Willow climbed into the passenger side of Clair's BMW. I took my place in the back seat. When we were buckled in, Clair performed a quick U-turn and drove us to the middle of town.

As Clair parallel parked in a space across from The Caffeinated Cup, I saw Willow's son sitting at a table near the front window. Willow was out of the car and across the street before we managed to open our doors.

When we caught up, the tiny elderly woman was strutting around like the chairman of the board. Willow had directed Johnny to change tables because she'd invited her friends. We all collected coffee and found a table for four at the back of the shop.

Johnny assessed our little group. "What's going on, Mom? I drove all the way here because you said it was important and now you've invited your friends for coffee."

He tipped his head to Clair and me. "No offence, but I took off work and hurried right over."

I shrugged and forced a weak smile. "No offense

taken."

I stole a glance at Clair, whose furrowed brow told me she was questioning our decision to join Willow. While I'd been willing to encourage the woman, I wondered at the wisdom of it now. I had no idea what she had planned. Some of her unorthodox ideas were coming back to me.

Willow wrapped both hands around her coffee and began. "Johnny, you're my son and I don't want to spend my last days on this earth arguing. Since you are so intent on my selling the house, that's what I will do."

Clair smiled. I almost fell out of my chair with the relief. Willow sounded completely rational.

Johnny let out a breath and grinned. "That's great. I can't tell you how happy it makes me, Mother. I'm convinced it's the best decision. I know you'll be happy at the Clairmont."

Willow held up a hand and raised her voice. "Hold on. I'm not finished. There are conditions. The town can have the house and the land it is on. But they can't have the side yard that holds my gazebo. I'll retain ownership of that property."

She pointed an index finger at her son. "When I die, you'll inherit it."

Johnny looked as confused as I felt. "Let me get this straight. You want to keep the gazebo now, but you'll leave it to me in your will."

His mother gave him a small smile. "Yes. But listen, I'm not finished. Although you will own the side yard and gazebo after I die, I don't want you to do anything with the property for fifty years. You can't disturb it and whoever might inherit it from you— should you die—must leave it alone for the duration of that specified time. After the fifty years are up, I don't care what they do with it." She eyed each of us, one by one. "You all understand?"

Clair and I stared back at her, wide-eyed.

Johnny sputtered. "Wait. Let's talk about this. It doesn't make sense. Do you understand what it would entail? If you keep possession of the gazebo, you'll still be responsible for taking care of the property even though you'll live on the other side of town. Mowing, weeding. You'll have to take care of any repairs on the gazebo. That thing's getting old." He paused. "And after you die, I'll be responsible for it. I don't even live in Twin Fawn, so I'd have to hire someone."

Willow reached across the table and patted Johnny's hand. "You can afford to pay for lawn care on that little bit of land."

Willow's son slanted his gaze and opened his mouth. I prepared to hear convincing words of wisdom, but maybe he didn't have any. He closed his mouth.

Willow's voice grew louder, even though Johnny had the good sense not to argue with her. "I'm telling you, that's the only way I'll sell. Those are my terms. We'll go to my lawyer to draw up the contract."

Johnny leaned back in his chair and quietly drank his coffee. "I didn't know you had a lawyer."

"Of course, I do. Ronald B. Ginsberg. His office is on Main Street."

"Oh." Was all Johnny said.

Willow squinted at him. "I know what you're thinking. I can see the wheels turning. You think you'll just wait for me to die and then sell the whole thing to the town council. But I'm putting it in the contract whether you agree or not. Fifty years!"

Johnny stayed quiet, so Willow went on and upped the anti. "Agree to my terms. If you fight me on it, I will be broken hearted for the rest of my life. I'm having Ginsberg put everything in my will. And if you try to break the will after I die, you will have broken your mother's heart beyond the grave. So, I want you to meet me at the lawyer's office. Sign papers that the property is not touched for at least fifty years."

Johnny began to sputter again. "Mother, I wouldn't go against your wishes. That's not what I was thinking."

"Then what was in your mind?"

I wondered if he was about to faint. He flapped a hand. "Um. I don't know. I'm just a little confused."

Willow calmly finished her coffee, set her mug down, and slid her chair out. "Tell you what. I'll give you an hour to think about it. Meet me at Ginsberg's office in an hour. If you are there, we'll sign the papers allowing the sale of the house but not the side yard with the gazebo. If you aren't there, I'll have him change my will, assuring that the property is protected. And you will have broken my heart."

Clair and I were as speechless as Johnny when Willow stood up and marched out of the Caffeinated Cup.

Clair jumped from the table and ran after Willow. "Wait, I'll unlock the BMW."

I stared at Johnny while I slid my chair away from the table. "Okay then. Nice to see you."

I sauntered after Clair, smiling and nodding greetings to other coffee shop customers while they stared wide eyed.

Upon reaching the sidewalk I'd concluded that the

elderly woman was a formidable opponent, and possibly insane.

Chapter Nine

"Good morning, world." I shuffled from the kitchen, juggling my first cup of coffee and a couple pieces of toast.

"Good morning." My mother, already dressed in jeans and hooded denim jacket—new style choice since Jack had arrived on the scene—finished with breakfast, and full of energy, scurried past me toward the front door. She always seemed to be on her way somewhere or returning from somewhere else. The oddities of our individual schedules made for a good roommate relationship. We passed each other in our daily activities but rarely tripped over one another.

Mom stopped at the door. "I haven't heard anything about Willow Ottenweller for a while. What's been happening since she laid down the law with Johnny? Is the sale going through? No more arguments about the gazebo?"

"It's been a month and they both seem pleased with the arrangement. I saw Willow at the Caffeinated Cup and spoke to her briefly. She appeared happy. Talked about getting moved into her new apartment and how she would arrange her furniture."

My mother smiled. "I'm so glad they got the

disagreement settled. It must be heartbreaking to be at odds with a child. Johnny's a good boy. He made a huge concession in agreeing to the gazebo fiasco." Mom hesitated with her hand on the knob. "It struck me as a drastic change of mind when Willow gave up the house. But it must be the gazebo that holds the strong emotional ties."

She shrugged and opened the door. "We all have things that mean a lot to us personally. Maybe not to anyone else, but they hold a special place in our heart."

On my way to work I stopped at The Caffeinated Cup to pick up scones to share with Mr. Bennett. The man loved his pastry. It was a short distance from the coffee shop to the hardware store, and I had almost made it there when I heard the tapping of high-heels. With slight dread I glanced behind me. One of the few heel-wearing women in town, Lovey Henderson, came strutting toward me. I thought of grabbing for the door handle and hustling inside. But she hailed me and obviously knew I'd seen her. How rude would it appear if I escaped inside? I stopped. What else could I do? There was no faking failure to see or hear her, so I smiled a greeting.

Typical of Lovey, she had so much to say she began a conversation while still a few steps away. "I'm so happy, today, I can't contain it. Isn't it wonderful? By spring, Twin Fawn will have a brand-new play park for the children and a lovely area for adults. Our town is moving up in the world. It'll have a big-city vibe before we know it."

I thought Twin Fawn would have miles to go before it approached any kind of city atmosphere. "I'm not sure what you're talking about. Have I missed something?"

"I'm talking about the expansion of Bird Song Park, of course."

"Oh. It's a small expansion but a nice addition. I still feel sorry for Mrs. Ottenweller having to give up her house but she seems to be doing alright, now."

Lovey went on. "My aunt lives near there and the whole neighborhood will be happy to get rid of the eyesore. She says the crazy old lady is still working on the plants around that old beat-up gazebo. Quite a waste of time, wouldn't you say? They'll all be gone when the town takes possession. Daddy says it'll only take a few days for the land movers to clear out all the old plants if the weather holds out. Maybe they'll even pour the concrete. Then in the spring all the new upscale playground equipment will arrive. I've been telling him we'll need rose gardens like Indianapolis. You've probably never seen the gardens in the state capital. I visit regularly. They are beautiful."

"I wouldn't think they could fit both the playground and rose gardens. The house is big but it won't leave that much space."

She leaned forward and spoke slowly and distinctly. "But the two lots—the house and the side yard—will provide plenty of room"

Proud of myself for having the upper-hand, I spoke distinctly, too. "The side yard won't be available for fifty years. It's the only way Willow would agree to the sale. It's in the contract. I was there when Willow and Johnny struck the bargain."

Lovey giggled and laid a cold clammy hand on my arm. "Don't tell me you fell for that foolishness. I guess I can't blame you, though. I get the information before anyone else in town. You know my daddy is on the town council. They would never let that woman keep the gazebo. They'll be tearing the ugly thing down and bulldozing all the old weedy gardens to make room for all the new equipment."

Her eyes got big and she slapped a hand over her mouth. "Oh, my goodness. Daddy told me to keep it a secret until it's done. He's going to kill me. You won't say anything will you?"

"I find that hard to believe. The land belongs to Willow Ottenweller. How could the town take it away from her?"

"I really shouldn't say anything, but it's just you. Pretty soon it won't matter anyway. The old woman's son, Johnny, started proceedings to have her declared unfit. I think they said something about mentally diminished or something. He's keeping it quiet until they get her moved. We don't want to upset the poor old thing, do we? Who knows what she would do. I'm sure you've heard all her ravings. She really can't be trusted to live alone."

I was losing ground, but needed to continue the fight. "But I thought it was all agreed when her son signed the papers protecting the gazebo."

Lovely issued a shrill unpleasant giggle. "He did that to pacify her. Johnny's being assigned as her guardian. When that goes through, any document she has signed will be null and void. It's obvious that no sane person would want that old beat-up building hanging around for another fifty years." She eyed me as if I might be that insane person.

"As if the judge would need any more proof, there are plenty of witnesses to her Bigfoot ramblings. You must have heard her crazy ideas, as well. It's a shame it all has to be done behind her back, but who knows how she will react? She might become violent."

I stared at Lovey Henderson in her baby blue coat and her high heeled shoes and her overly blond hair, and steamed inwardly, but couldn't find the words to continue the argument.

She raised her wrist to display a bejeweled watch. "Look at the time." She gave me one of her toothy, fake smiles. "I must get to my dress shop. They'll be wondering where I am. I'm sure you have somewhere to be, too."

She walked away, and I stood stunned for a moment before grabbing the door knob to let myself into Bennett's Hardware. I dumped the scones next to the coffee pot and retreated to my office to think.

Poor Willow. She might have a screw loose—or several screws loose—but was it fair to keep her in the dark regarding proceedings that would change her life? Looking at it from Johnny's point of view, I understood his frustration. Was it the only course of action that made sense?

I could only hope Willow would find a way to accept the decision and move on with life at Clairmont.

But how would she react when she learned of Johnny's intentions? Would she label it treachery? I covered my face with my hands to keep from screaming. Every course of action that came to mind seemed to end in disaster for someone.

What if Lovey Henderson wasn't as wrong as I wanted her to be?

Was Willow capable of violence?

Chapter Ten

Worrying never fixed a problem. My father's words of wisdom circulated in my mind. Unfortunately, I'd be unable to fix Willow's problems with or without the worry. I needed to set the turmoil surrounding her aside and enjoy the peace for a while. It was time to take a day off from being a fixer and do something for myself. My first mundane task would be to arrange a ride to pick up my car from the repair shop so I could spend the day browsing antique shops.

I found my mother in the laundry room, arms reaching deep inside the clothes dryer. "Mom, they called to tell me my car is ready."

She pulled back and stood up, having retrieved a sweatshirt. "Did they find the problem?"

"All fixed and ready to go. There's one hitch. They can't deliver it until later in the day and I don't want to be stuck here with no wheels. Can you give me a ride to pick it up?"

Mom pulled on the sweatshirt and zipped it up. "I'm sorry, dear. Don't you remember that I loaned your brother my car for the day? I'm riding with Jack on a job, and he'll be here any minute." She walked to the door to peer out the window.

Harumph. "Chad and Julie need to get another car. I don't know how they get along with only one." That was another thing I didn't want to worry about.

"Would Jack mind dropping me at the garage?"

"Dear, you know he always goes out of his way to help, but the repair shop is on the other side of town, and I'd hate to make him late. Maybe you could stay home and read a book."

I felt like stamping my foot, but I put on my sad face instead. The face had been a valuable asset when I was in middle school. As an adult, it wasn't as effective.

After a moment's pause, my mother grabbed her phone and hit one of her saved numbers. While the call connected, she said, "I'm calling Garrett. I bet he'd be happy to give you a lift."

No! I reached out with thoughts of ripping the phone from her hand. But she held up her other hand and smiled. Garrett was on the line.

I hissed at my mother. "I don't want to presume on Garrett. I'm sure he has better things to do than taxi me around." Mom wasn't listening. She was chatting to Garrett about the weather. I stood in front of her waving my hands and whispering. "Stop. I'll call Uber."

She pulled the phone away from her face. "Silly. We don't have Uber in Twin Fawn."

Turning away from me, she spoke a few more words into the phone, then clicked it off. "Garrett will be right over." With the phone stuffed securely into her pocket she pulled a warm jacket from the hall closet.

I felt a thumping in my ears. "What do you mean he'll be right here? Right now? I have to change." I panicked, turned and ran up the stairs two at a time to get to my bedroom. I pulled a brush through my hair while rummaging through my closet.

My mother called from the bottom of the stairs. "You look fine, Liberty. You're only going to pick up the car. I'm sure the repairmen won't notice your attire."

After I pulled on my new blue sweater, I trotted back downstairs, checked the mirror, fluffed my hair, and applied lipstick."

Mom stood by the door with her hands on her hips. "What are you worried about? It's only Garrett. For goodness sakes, you've known him forever. You played in the sandbox with him, in nothing but your diaper!" She laughed and stepped out onto the porch.

"Thanks for the reminder and a mental image that will haunt me forever." For someone who considered herself an aspiring private detective, my mother could be clueless.

I paced from the living room to the front door watching for Garrett. As soon as his car showed up outside, I darted out the door, trotted to the drive and hopped into the passenger seat.

Words flew from my mouth as soon as I buckled the seat belt. "Thanks so much. I really appreciate the ride. My car was in for minor repair. Mom and your father are so busy with their new business, she didn't have time to give me a ride. I could have walked, but it's on the other side of town and quite a distance on foot. I hope you didn't feel pressured into this. My mother sometimes just assumes that people have nothing better to do than favors for her. I guess in this case it's a favor for me."

Lord, help me. Why was I babbling?

Garrett turned to me with his earthshaking smile

and answered in his smooth deep voice. "It's no problem at all. Actually, perfect timing. I had some things to do in town anyway."

"I'm so grateful. I…" I bit my tongue to stem the flow of nonsensical twitter."

After that, for fear of babbling again, I kept quiet. That made for an awkward silence until we were distracted by a little old lady waiting to cross the street. She had a cloud of white fuzz surrounding her face and her arms wrapped around a stuffed garbage bag. She stood at the corner shifting her weight from foot to foot.

Garrett pressed on the brake and pulled to the curb. "Isn't that Mrs. Ottenweller? She looks like she could use some help."

I liked this about Garrett. Always willing to help someone. No need to debate the pros and cons or whether he had time.

I pressed the down button on my window. "Willow, how are you? That looks like quite a burden. Where are you heading?"

She let the bag slide down to the sidewalk. "I'm taking this over to my house for the moving sale. I've collected so much junk over the years and had the silly idea I could fit most of it into my apartment. Of course, there isn't near enough room for it."

"Downsizing can be tough. You're smart to be sorting through it. You'll have more space for your new adventure."

Willow nodded and lifted the bag again. Garrett leaned across me—wow, he smelled nice—and spoke through the window. "That's too far to walk. Hop in. We'll give you a ride."

Willow gave a weak smile and sighed. "Very kind

of you. I'd be grateful for the lift." Garrett was out and holding the door for her in a flash. Then he grabbed the bag and loaded it into the seat beside her.

"You kids are so helpful. I'm still getting used to arranging transportation since Johnny took my keys. I guess he's right. I'm too old to be driving. Dinged the car the last two times I drove it." She then entertained us with descriptions of her new home while we drove toward Bird Song Park.

As we approached the old mansion, it became apparent that Willow had company. Garrett slowed the car and the three of us stared at a cluster of people in Willow's yard. I twisted toward her. "Who are all those people? Are you having the sale, today?"

"Not until next week. What are they doing on my property? They're trespassing."

As Garrett pulled the car into the drive, Willow screeched, pushed her door open and tumbled out. "No! My gazebo!"

By the time we opened our doors, Willow had run half way to the side yard. I followed and saw the problem. A furry white dog bounced in and out of a muddy hole next to Willow's beloved gazebo. George Trainer stood in the mud grabbing for, and missing, the canine. To my surprise and consternation, my mother and Jack Reed stood at the side cheering George on.

As we approached, I recognized George's Westie, Riley, from previous descriptions of the run-away pooch. He joyfully burrowed deeper in while the dirt flew in all directions. George made a final lunge into the hole and came up caked with mud, but with Riley in his arms.

Garrett and I stopped beside my mother and Jack. I

had to ask. "What are you two doing here? Is this your case? Are you working for George?"

My mother answered. "No. We were on our way but got distracted when we saw George out combing the streets again. We couldn't help but volunteer to help him. His dog, Riley, is a rescue West Highland White. The guy can't seem to keep that dog on a leash. As you see, Riley's been found, but I guess we'll have to help George do a little repair work. Poor Willow is so attached to her gazebo."

I almost blurted the secret that Willow wouldn't have possession of that precious property for long, but decided I wouldn't join Lovey Henderson in her malicious gossip. Maybe Willow would still win the conflict.

As we drew closer and peered into the scene of the crime, Garrett laughed. "Look at the depth of the cavern. That dog is better than a backhoe at moving dirt."

George Trainer climbed from the pit holding the wiggling Westie. He raised his hand to Willow. "I'm so sorry. I discovered Riley was missing an hour ago and I've been searching everywhere. I had no idea he'd be all the way over here or I would have stopped him sooner." He scanned the damage. "I promise I'll fix this."

George carefully put Riley on the ground beside him and smiled. "Look at that. He's calm as a kitten now. Guess he wore himself out with all the running and digging."

Mom stepped up and put her arm around Willow. "We'll help George fill it in and replant your flowers."

Willow leaned over the hole, staring into it intently.

She became oddly calm and smiled sweetly at George. "No damage, George. It's alright." Then she addressed my mother. "No need for you to bother. I'll fill it myself."

I breathed a sigh of relief. Her plants, which she had often referred to as her children, were torn, battered, and scattered along the sides of the excavation. Yet, she showed no sign of previous hysterics. Had she finally lost her mind?

While George continued to offer new words of apology, I noticed the space beside his feet was vacant. The dog no longer sat at his side.

I whispered to my mother. "Where's Riley?"

She glanced around. "Oh, he's scampered off somewhere. He's quite a cantankerous canine."

Mom had barely finished her sentence when screams split the air around us. I looked at Willow, expecting a new fit of hysteria. But this time the squeals didn't come from her. A woman I recognized from the park, stood beside the house with her mouth wide open. One by one, spectators twisted toward the house, searching out the source of the racket.

The screams came from the woman, but the problem had formed closer to the ground. Dirt flew from the center of a new crater, and mounded up all around. I shot a glance at Willow, expecting an explosion of elderly screams. She seemed calm, while the newcomer continued to shriek.

"What's that dog doing now?" George took off at a trot toward the newly developing offense. As he arrived at the excavation, his dog hopped out, proudly dragging a trophy.

"Darn it, Riley, what am I going to do with you?"

George grabbed one end of the stick the dog carried, and pulled. "Drop it." Riley enjoyed a short game of tug-of-war before finally releasing it. George breathed a sigh of relief and held up Riley's prize. "The dog found a stick....or something." His face blanched white and he propelled Riley's find back into the hole. The new toy was not a stick.

I approached cautiously, surrounded by a few of the more quizzical onlookers. We found a sight that caused us all to turn white. The squealing woman had silenced. I heard only gasps as each spectator recognized the trophy Riley had unearthed.

Jack pulled his cell phone from his pocket and punched in the three-digit emergency number. With the voice of authority, he said, "Send someone over to Willow Ottenweller's house. It's the big place beside Bird Song Park." He paused. "What's the emergency? Well, it looks like we've found human remains. A dog just unearthed bones in the yard."

He paused. "No. I'm pretty sure they are human. The dog pulled out what looks like a tibia. Might be a full skeleton in there. No hurry. Whoever it is, or was, has been dead for some time."

Human bones. I opted to take Jack's word for it and stopped short of a clear view. The leg bone was enough. I'd never seen a dead body or a real skeleton and didn't care to see one now. My mother, on the other hand, edged closer and stared at it intently.

Neighbors came out of their homes and the crowd of onlookers grew as we waited for the police. Most reacted as I expected. Women covered their faces or turned away. Men pointed and shook their heads. Kids had to be pulled away and sent home.

Willow's reaction surprised me. I thought she would at least be upset over the digging, if not the dead person in the hole. Instead, she stared into it, then turned to gaze at the gazebo, then shifted her attention back to the hole beside the house. Her lips moved but very little sound came out.

Had the shock pushed her over the edge? Fearing she might resume the hysterics I moved closer to her and worked at deciphering barely audible muttering.

She mumbled. "But what are they doing over here?" She put her fingers to her chin and looked at the bones. She pushed wispy white hair from her face and turned toward the gazebo and whispered. "It isn't right."

I leaned toward her and spoke softly. "What do you mean? Are you feeling okay?"

Startled, almost as if she'd forgotten we were all standing there, she smiled at me. "It's nothing, dear."

"Do you know who might be buried on your property?"

"No! Of course not. Why would you even think there would be anyone buried in my yard."

I pointed to the crater. Her gaze shifted to it and then back to the gazebo.

The police arrived and began their work.

After a brief assessment, Officer Arnie approached Willow. "Mrs. Ottenweller, I'll take you to the station to be interviewed. You'll be more comfortable there."

The old woman jerked back a few inches and gazed at him. "You're that policeman who wouldn't pay attention when I called you about the Crosley creature. You thought I was a silly old woman. Now you want to talk to me. Why should I help you? I've nothing to do with it."

The officer stammered. "Well...Willow. Um, Mrs. Ottenweller. We'll need your statement. Because there's definitely a dead body buried in your yard."

My mother had always taken the responsibility for comforting Twin Fawn citizens. I looked for her but found her deep in conversation with one of the bystanders. It fell to me to whisper words of encouragement to Willow. I prepared myself. She seemed confused but not frail. What would I do if she became combative?

I tried to recall how these things were handled on television, softened my voice, put a smile in it. "Don't worry. I wouldn't want to ride in the squad car, either. Garrett and I will drive you to the police station, and we'll stay for the interview. Okay?"

She glanced up at me. "Thank you. That would be nice. I really don't know anything about whatever is in that hole, though."

Before I could guide Willow to Garrett's car, another piercing shriek hurt my ears. I stomped my foot and turned toward the noise, ready to scold somebody. "For goodness sakes. Who is it now?" I'd assumed any hysterics were exhausted. My nerves could only put up with so many squeals in one day.

Lovey Henderson barreled past me and fell onto Garrett's shoulder. She had shown up on the scene in time to send up a wail before the police covered the skeleton. With her arms wrapped around his neck, she played the perfect soap opera love interest. "Oh, Garrett. I was passing by and saw all the activity so I stopped. I wish I hadn't. I wish I'd never seen this. It's horrible." She let out an extended sob. "I think I might faint."

How dramatic could the woman be? Her eye make-up hadn't even smudged.

The whining continued. "I can't get the sight of it out of my mind. Please take me home." She looked into his eyes and shook her head. "I shouldn't drive."

Garrett snugged his arm around Lovey. "Of course, honey. Just a sec." He called to his father. "Would you drive Libby and Willow to the police station?"

My mother suddenly became very helpful, failing to read the scowl on my face. "Yes, of course we will." She rushed to Willow's side. "I'll call Johnny. He should be with you."

Willow shook her head. "No. Don't bother him. He'll be at work and it's too far to drive."

"Well, whatever you say. You may want him to be with you later. Just let me know." She put an arm around Willow's shoulders. "Come with me. Jack's car is right over here." I trailed behind and climbed into the back seat with Willow.

The little woman remained quiet and stared out the window for most of the journey. We were about two blocks from the station when she began to breathe heavily and the mummering began again. I leaned in to listen. "Why there? Wrong. All wrong."

My mother and Jack were in conversation in the front and paying no attention to the possible danger in the back. That's when I began my own mumbling, praying Willow would remain calm until we arrived at the station, and I was no longer trapped in the backseat with her.

The transition from the car to the interview room at the station brought Willow back to reality. She remained quiet while we waited for a police officer to find time to speak to her. I occupied the time by peering through a window in the door, watching officers rush about. My mother did her best to entertain Willow with nonsensical ramblings.

At one point, Officer Arnie stepped into the room. "Good news. They've found the wallet. It was pretty beat-up, but the contents were legible. As we suspected it belonged to Harley Ottenweller. So, it's a good bet that those are the bones of your husband, Mrs. Ottenweller."

Willow numbly nodded. "Yes. I thought I recognized the clothes." She raised her chin quickly. "But I don't know how he got there."

The officer nodded to her. "Yes ma'am. Someone will be with you shortly." Arnie paused on his way to the door. "Um. I'm sorry for your loss."

After he left the room, I mulled over the incoherent ramblings of a confused old woman and questioned her final straight forward declaration.

The hours passed with the occasional interruption of a policeman stepping in to ask a question. I suspected my mother had phoned Johnny, because at some point he arrived. He rushed into the room and grabbed Willow's hands. "Don't worry, this is a terrible mistake. I'll talk to the police and take care of this."

Before he could release Willow's hands, a policeman opened the door and leaned in. "We need to speak to you, Mr. Ottenweller. Would you step out into the hall?"

"No! Leave him alone." Willow sprang to her feet sending her chair slamming into the wall. In continuous motion, she lunged and attached herself to the officer's arm.

I figured I should do something but the man seemed able to take care of himself. He stood a good two feet taller than Willow.

The tiny woman demanded the policeman's attention. "I did it. I shot Harley Ottenweller and buried him out there, years ago. He was a mean man. I couldn't stand it anymore, so I shot him. Then I buried him under the gazebo. Er. I mean next to the house."

The officer carefully stripped Willow's fingers from his arm. "Which was it? You buried him next to the gazebo or next to the house?"

With her hands stiffly at her sides she gave him a stern stare. "The house of course. That's where you found him wasn't it? I just forgot. It was a stressful time. But I did it. I want to write a confession right now. Give me some paper." She glanced around the room. "Who's got a pen?"

The officer picked up her chair and returned it to its original position, then guided Willow back to the table. "Mrs. Ottenweller. Have a seat and someone will be in to talk to you." He left the room, taking Johnny with him. He spoke to another officer out in the hall, then sent Johnny back in.

Willow's son pulled a chair close to his mother. "This is ridiculous. You could never kill anything. Not a bug. Not even a rat, let alone your husband. You know you've been…imagining things."

Willow crossed her arms and stared at the wall. "I did it."

Johnny put an arm around her shoulders. "You're confused. You didn't kill anyone."

"I'm confessing. I know what I'm doing. You go

on home now, let the police take care of things." She calmly settled back in her seat. "You'll want to call and cancel my lease at the retirement village. I won't be needing the apartment."

The rest of the day passed in a blur. At the end, Willow was installed in a cell.

We all protested vigorously, but without success. Officer Arnie explained. "I didn't want to hold her. She refused to leave and insisted we arrest her. So, tonight, she's our guest. I'll make sure she has a couple blankets and pillows. Maybe a cup of tea."

~~

I woke up early the next day with Willow on my mind but Jack suggested I wait until afternoon before I visited her at the station. "They'll have the stories straightened out by then and you or Johnny can take her home."

When I got there, I hoped to hear that she'd recanted her confession. She sat in the same room where we had spent so much time the day before and pulled up a chair beside her. I greeted her as warmly as I could. "What do the police say? Can we take you home, now?"

Willow smiled at me. "I killed him."

I guessed there was still more story straightening to do. Within a few minutes, a police officer entered carrying a stack of papers. "Mrs. Ottenweller, we know you didn't shoot your husband."

"I did too."

"No ma'am. The doctor checked out the remains. He said Harley wasn't shot at all. There were no bullet holes, no bullets or spent shells. He died of blunt force trauma. Someone bashed him in the head."

"What?" Willow's forehead wrinkled, and her chin trembled for a moment. She finally took a deep breath. "Oh, that's right. I hit him with a rock. A big rock. It was handy."

The police officer pulled out a chair and sat at the table. "Why do you keep confessing? First, you were confused about where he was buried, and then you didn't know how he died." His voice turned stern. "You're wasting our time."

I knew Willow was tough. She also proved resilient. She sounded as clear headed as any lawyer when she answered him. "Officer, I can't be expected to remember everything. It's your job to figure these things out. I'm old." She shrugged. "I forget things. Doesn't change the fact that I killed him."

Willow leaned across the table to stare the officer in the eye. "Now listen, I signed the paper. If you need another, since I got the modus operandi wrong, I'll sign another confession. It's gonna say the same thing. I killed him."

The officer stretched his arms toward the ceiling and groaned.

Johnny had arrived at the station during this time, and seeing him through the window, Willow rushed to his side. She latched onto his arm and attempted to drag him out of the building. "What are you doing here? Go home. Your family needs you."

To fulfill my job as encourager, I followed hoping to offer a few calming words. So far, I was at a loss for inspiration but kept watch by hovering behind the policemen as they gathered.

Johnny planted his feet and even feisty Willow couldn't budge him. "Mom, stop this craziness. I know you didn't kill Dad."

Willow shot glances at the policemen who had now surrounded them. I peeked between the uniformed bodies. She moved closer to Johnny and hissed. "I won't let you go to jail for his death. You were just a boy and he was a mean man. What you did was as much for me as for yourself. So, go home and let me do this."

Johnny's voice raised an octave. "What do you mean? I didn't kill Dad. How could you think that?"

She whispered. "Good. Keep that up. I know what happened. You buried him there and built that gazebo to cover it." She shook her head. "Or you buried him next to the house. Then the gazebo construction drew attention away from your digging the grave next to the house." She smiled at him and patted his shoulder. "Good strategy."

She glanced over her shoulder at me. "He always was a smart boy."

Officer Arnie took Willow gently by the arm. "Come with me. You are going back to your cell until we get this figured out."

She gazed up at him. "I killed Harley Ottenweller."

A tight smile formed on Arnie's face. Or it could have been that he was gritting his teeth. Then he nodded. "Yes, Mrs. Ottenweller."

Chapter Eleven

Clair swirled her coffee while I played with the trailing vines of the coffee shop's potted Tradescantia Zebrina. The vines had grown in the last few weeks and now brushed the table. I thought how nice that the plant thrived in the sunny window and peaceful atmosphere. It was so much like me in that regard.

My friend placed her cup on the table. "The whole town's talking about Willow Ottenweller, the little old woman who killed her husband and then hid the crime for years. People are saying all her problems stem from the crime. Speculation is that the weight of years of guilt made her crazy and even produced the hallucinations. For instance—the Crosley Monster and talking plants."

I decided not to mention my imagined kinship with the happy Tradescantia Zebrina. "Willow didn't actually say her plants talked. Only that they might rebel." I realized this was a weak defense and I wouldn't make much of a witness.

Clair pushed her chair away from the table and trotted to the coffee counter. "I need a warm-up." From there, she raised her voice to continue our conversation.

"I'm worried about little Willow sitting in jail with no family close-by."

The waitress, Ella, topped off Clair's coffee and took the opportunity to join in. "She sure didn't look like a murderer. Or is it murderess? Whatever, she seemed to be harmless." Looking Clair in the eye, she continued, "I guess you can never tell. I watch true crime shows on television." She subtly waved a hand at the room. "A serial killer could be sitting at one of these tables, drinking coffee and chewing on a scone."

"Yikes. I watch those shows, too." Clair shot a glance around the room and scurried back to her seat across from me.

I called across the distance between the table and the coffee counter. "Ella, I don't believe Willow killed anyone. And she certainly isn't a serial killer. The poor thing is obviously confused. There were too many flaws in her story to make her confession credible." I made an effort to sound authoritative, but in truth, what did I know about killers?

I touched Clair's arm and whispered. "We should keep our voices down. Whatever we say will be all over Twin Fawn in no time. And we will be misquoted."

Clair leaned toward me, effectively cutting Ella and everyone else out of the conversation. "How long do you think they'll keep Willow in jail?"

I lifted my shoulders. "I have no idea. I worried about her at first, but now I'm thinking it may be for the best. She's comfortable and in a safe place. When I visited the jail, she seemed happy. She's only been there three days and has already made herself at home. I took in her knitting and a potted plant."

Clair tipped her head. "I guess if they let her have

the knitting needles, Officer Arnie must believe she's harmless. But I wonder how many inmates keep plants in their cell."

"Willow loves her plants and I wanted her cell to feel cozy. She'll have a little friend to take care of."

Clair simply nodded. "Un huh."

I paused to slurp my coffee. "So, back to the whole murder fiasco. What are we to believe? Willow sounded completely rational as she confessed to killing Harley. Except for getting the details wrong. Then, I heard her accuse Johnny of the crime."

Clair put an elbow on the table and propped her chin on her hand. "Do you think Johnny could have killed his father? Because, if he did, Willow would want to protect him. That would explain her insistence on her own guilt."

I shook my head. "No way."

Had I answered too quickly? I paused to think it through, but came up with the same conclusion. "If he'd killed someone at age thirteen, don't you think there would have been signs? I think he would have turned psycho by now."

"I don't know the guy. The sale of Willow's house didn't go through our office. Are you sure there were never signs? No sinister activity? No missing pets or playmates?" She put up a hand. "Just kidding about the playmates. We would have heard through the gossip train."

"I guess I don't know him either. He was a year or two ahead of me in school and left Twin Fawn after graduation. I've only met him at Bennett's Hardware when he came in with his mother."

I downed the last dregs of my coffee and picked up

the bag of scones I'd purchased. "Enough stewing over this, today. One of my mother's favorite descriptive terms for sitting in worry and cultivating anxiety." I smiled at the thought. "I'm off to work. Talk to you later."

I walked out the door determined to think of pleasant things, but the short distance to the hardware store had me lost in thought about Willow and Johnny. Yep, Mom would say I was stewing. Willow didn't seem to be suffering in her cell, but she couldn't stay in the friendly Twin Fawn Police Station forever. What could I do to help her when she refused to help herself? Refused even when everyone who knew her, including her son, begged her to recant the confession."

I've never been a suspicious person, so I guess no one would call me a great judge of character. But nowhere in my imagination did I picture Willow as a murderer. Or as Ella had said, murderess? I hesitated to place the blame on Johnny, as well.

The fact remained someone had indeed killed Harley Ottenweller and might still walk the streets of Twin Fawn. Someone buried Harley's bones on Willow's property. How could she have missed someone digging a hole behind her house? It seemed probable the sweet woman was covering for someone. But who?

I'd almost reached the hardware when I heard a raspy voiced call. "Ho, Liberty." Working on placing the voice, I spun to see Oscar White limping up behind me, leaning on his cane with every step. Oscar, a long-time resident of Twin Fawn, had been an imposing presence for as long as I could remember. The man attended every town meeting, every high school athletic event, holiday celebration, most funerals and any other gathering involving ten or more citizens. Anytime you wanted an opinion on any town happening, you could ask Oscar. When you didn't ask, he would give you his judgment anyway, if you were unlucky enough to get yourself cornered.

Today, I'd been cornered.

"Hey, Oscar. How are you?" Obesity and lumbago hindered his stride, so I obligingly waited for the elderly gentleman as he navigated the last few feet separating us. I glanced longingly at the door of the hardware, only about six feet away. So close, yet so far. I was not in the mood for a long conversation, but if I continued into the store, he'd follow. Then Mr. Bennett would be drawn into whatever Oscar had on his mind. I liked my boss too much to do that to him.

Oscar came up beside me, puffing a bit. "Isn't this...weather pleasant?"

The weather was not particularly pleasant. I guessed he wanted to talk about something else. "Yes, but it's a bit chilly for my taste." Might as well get it over with. I reached for a friendly smile. "What brings you out this morning?"

He waved a hand that seemed to include the entire Main Street retail area. "This thing about Willow Ottenweller is wrong. It's bad for business. They've put her in jail for murder. A disgrace. Willow's an elderly woman who has lost her mind. She's bugged out. Gone cuckoo. Everyone knows that."

I wouldn't have been so judgmental about Willow if I were Oscar. I calculated his age to be about the same as Willow's and had often wondered about the state of his mind.

He continued. "I've been an integral part of the Twin Fawn community my entire life, and I remember when Harley took off. At least we thought he'd skipped town, at the time. Couldn't believe he left such a beautiful woman. She was a good wife and mother. Turns out something happened to him, but I never saw any sign of mischief at the time. I even helped the Ottenweller boy build that gazebo right afterward. Spent enough time there I'd have seen any hint of wrongdoing."

He paused to scan the street, and returned his attention to me. "If you ask me, they should put those bones back into the ground—in the cemetery, of course—and forget the whole thing. Willow Ottenweller has been through enough. She needs care not incarceration. And what if she did do it? Nobody would've blamed her. Besides, the woman's too far gone to prosecute."

At this point I took a half step back because Oscar pointed an index finger at me. "A petition. That's what we need. A petition to show community support. Get the whole town to sign. Our so-called law enforcement will have no choice but to let her go. Why don't you type something up and start circulating it?"

My weak little mouse voice squeaked out. "Me?"

He nodded. "Yeah. I'll help you with the wording, of course. Then all you'll need is to take it house to house. Start at one side of town and work your way to the other. Get everyone's signature."

The little mouse voice in my head kept whispering, 'Think fast, Liberty.' Surprisingly, a strategy did pop into my head. "That's a great idea, Oscar, but who would listen to me? You're the obvious choice. Is there anyone so well respected? You are a pillar of the community. It's obvious that you're the most qualified person to get that petition signed."

Oscar pushed on his cane and stood a little straighter. "I've noticed people look for my guidance on important matters. I'd hate to let them down." He nodded at me, did an about face, and limped away, calling over his shoulder. "I'll work on it."

With a wave of relief, I slid into the hardware shop and dumped the scones on the counter beside the coffee pot. Then I retreated to my office to ponder town politics. Oscar White was a boorish man, but he seemed to care about Willow, or he had at one time. I hadn't noticed he showed so much concern for others in town. Was his interest more than neighborly friendship? If there'd been gossip about the two, I hadn't heard.

Mr. Bennett stood at the office door with a scone in his hand and a satisfied smile on his face. I asked what he thought of Oscar White.

He took time to swallow a bite of scone. "He's fine as long as I don't have to talk to him. Thinks he runs the town. He's a bully. Always has been."

"Is he married?"

"Yes, at one time, but she left him years ago. I don't remember him even having a lady friend after that. But what woman would put up with him?"

Mr. Bennett took time to brush crumbs from his shirt. "I remember a time when he hung around the Ottenweller house. Right after Harley disappeared. Some of us thought he had a thing for Willow, but she must have made it clear she wasn't interested. After a while we didn't see him over there."

My boss finished his scone and returned to the

sales floor. I sat wondering at the depth of Oscar White's interest in Willow Ottenweller.

Chapter Twelve

Bird Song Park had lost its appeal when it came to leisurely afternoon walks. The breeze stung my skin and seemed colder than the temperature warranted. And as for pleasant surroundings, a walk would inevitably take me past Willow Ottenweller's house. The big old mansion sat dark and empty. Sticks and dead leaves littered the yard. The little lady, who loved it, remained in jail. No one raked leaves or picked up debris. Even neighbors, who normally would have been happy to help her care for her lawn, shunned it. I suppose no one wanted to think of having lived so near a murderer these past years. Were they wondering what sinister traits they may have missed?

How could I blame them when I found it easier, myself, to avoid the area and drive straight home after work. I'd formed a habit of lounging in front of the television to fill the time before dinner.

On this day, I arrived home surprised at the sound of voices. I poked my head into the living room to see what was going on. Officer Arnie sat on my couch nursing a cup of coffee. He wore his blue uniform. His hat lay on the sofa beside him. My mother and Jack occupied two side chairs, leaning in, engrossed in dynamic conversation.

Mom glanced my way. "Liberty, I'm glad you're home. Come join us. We've been discussing this matter up one side and down the other, without success. Another point of view would be invaluable."

"Sure. What's up?" I may have sounded enthusiastic, but I knew better than to count on sharing my thoughts. When Mom and Jack were discussing anything, finding the space to insert a spare word tended to be a rare occurrence. I edged past Arnie and plopped into the recliner.

"Sad news, I'm afraid." My mother began. "Arnie tells us that Willow Ottenweller is almost certain to be formally charged with Harley's murder."

The big man shrugged and carefully set down the fragile flowered coffee cup my mother had provided. "I never believed she did it, but I've done everything I can think of to get the truth from her." He slapped the coffee table. "The blessed woman keeps confessing to the crime. Every time we tell her she got it wrong, she alters her confession to fit the facts."

The officer slumped back against the couch. "I'm frustrated. It isn't easy to investigate other suspects when Willow takes all the credit." He paused and blew out a breath. "The truth is, I'm beginning to believe she really did murder him. We all know she has her eccentricities. Is it possible her memory is so poor she can't remember exactly how she killed him, just that she did?"

Mom shook her head and ran fingers through her gray hair. "I can't accept it. She's never been the kind of person who could commit any crime, let alone a murder. And then to keep it a secret for so long."

She reached out and patted the officer's knee. "But I understand your position. I'm at as much of a loss as you are."

Mom turned adoring eyes to Jack. "Can you think of anything else? There must be something we haven't thought of."

Jack glanced at Arnie. "What about her son? Is there any suspicion Johnny could have done it? Afterall, at thirteen, boys can be unpredictable. All those hormones coursing through their bodies. If he thought Harley was hurting his mother, he might have lost control. Boys at that age don't have much self-control to begin with."

Arnie wrapped his hands around his coffee cup. "We looked into his whereabouts and checked out what he was doing at the time. First, we had to determine the approximate date Harley came up missing. You remember his disappearance was never reported. The doc can't pinpoint an exact time of death. All we have to go on is a conversation between Mrs. Ottenweller and a neighbor. The neighbor recalls Willow complaining her husband left without acknowledging their anniversary, so we got the date. She said he didn't come home that day or the next. The neighbor remembers Willow being very upset about it. I guess even a husband who is a jerk, is expected to celebrate an anniversary."

Arnie gave a short laugh. "The neighbor reported that after those two days, she couldn't say if Harley had returned home or not. She had always avoided him as much as possible and made every effort not to see him. That's pretty much what everyone said when we asked." Arnie paused to tip up his cup and found it empty. My mother grabbed it and trotted to the kitchen. She took only a moment to return the refilled cup to the police officer.

"Thank you, Mrs. Cassell. This is good coffee." He gave her a big smile and continued. "So, using that timeline, it turns out that Johnny was at Adventure Camp with about twenty other boys. They were camping at Crosley State Fish and Wildlife Area. Half of those boys still live in Twin Fawn, and several were able to confirm Johnny was probably with them. Their memories weren't so good, but from their testimonies we think it's unlikely Johnny Ottenweller had anything to do with Harley's disappearance. By the time the group had returned home, Harley hadn't been seen for at least two days."

As expected, no one asked my opinion on the matter. It seemed they had all points covered, and it all led back to Willow. The little elderly woman seemed determined and destined to go to prison for killing Harley Ottenweller.

With all speculation exhausted, we sat quietly drinking coffee. While no one seriously believed Willow had killed her husband, we were becoming resigned to the fact she'd be charged with the crime.

Arnie finished his coffee, graciously turned down my mother's invitation to stay for dinner, and left us.

~~

Bright and early the next morning, I went to see Willow. I'd given up trying to persuade her to change her story. This time I visited solely to encourage. Simple conversation, meant to help shorten the hours of being alone in the cell. I practiced on the way there.

'How are they treating you here?' 'Do you need me to bring you anything from home?' 'What are you knitting?'

She smiled in her sweet contented way. "I'm perfectly comfortable here. Everyone is so kind to me. I just wish they would stop trying to put the blame on someone else. I killed Harley and buried him. Those are the facts. I want to serve my sentence."

I pressed my lips together and nodded. "I'm not here to change your mind, only to keep you company for a while."

"You've been so nice to visit me. So many of my friends are standoffish now since they found out I killed Harley." She brightened and put down her knitting. "Funny thing. Oscar White came by to see me. That was certainly a surprise. We hadn't even spoken in years. He said he wanted to make sure they were making me comfortable. I guess you can't tell about people. It was nice of him to visit. He didn't stay long and didn't say much, but it was a nice thought."

I left the jail, all the more certain of Willow's innocence. I had no evidence, only a simple hunch, but I walked down the steps determined to try one last avenue.

Don't ask me why. I'd never wanted to be a detective or anything similar. I liked mystery movies and who-done-it shows but left it to the characters to discover the culprit. I had no sneaky strategy for solving this case. But one idea niggled at me. A stupid plan, but the only one I had.

There seemed to be one man who might have enough clout to save my friend. He knew the mayor and politicians in town and he could badger anyone enough to turn them to his way of thinking. After a walk down Main Street and back, I stopped in at the Caffeinated Cup, sat by the window and made one cup of coffee last for the next hour. When I figured Ella might ask me to purchase another coffee or leave, I vacated the table. It was time for another trek around town.

Just as I'd thought of giving up, I saw him. Oscar White hobbled down the sidewalk on the other side of the street. To the consternation of several drivers and the sound of honking horns, I dodged traffic and trotted up behind him.

I knew I'd have to monopolize the conversation. If he got started, I'd be lost. I spoke fast. "Oscar, I'm so glad I found you. Something terrible is about to happen. Have you heard? They've concluded Willow murdered Harley and are planning to send her to a woman's prison. Oh, maybe not a woman's prison. I think somebody told me it's an institution for the criminally insane."

I rolled my eyes and grimaced. "The place is known for feeding the inmates terrible food. Gruel, I think. The prisoners don't complain because they're given drugs every day to keep them quiet." At this point, I made a show of wringing my hands. "Can you imagine? It probably turns them into zombies." I paused to take a breath.

"And they're never allowed outside the building. That breaks my heart because you know how Willow loves being in nature. And what will she do without her gardening? She'll never be able to live like that. Imagine spending the rest of her life inside a prison, never seeing the light of day. And with crazy people. What will happen to her?"

Lies. Lies. I should be ashamed of myself and I planned to pray for forgiveness, later. I had no idea where Willow would serve her time. I'd made it all up. No one had said anything about an institution for the criminally insane, or being confined inside, or gruel, or drugs. I was stunned Oscar fell for it.

Oscar's eyes had widened as I spewed out fabrications. His skin had gone pasty, his breathing got shallow and, for a moment, I thought he might faint. But he recovered enough to turn and limp away, sputtering words I didn't understand.

I watched as he hobbled down the street hoping he'd be motivated to put up a fight for Willow. If he collapsed on the pavement, I'd have to call the emergency line. But mostly I prayed he might badger the police department or the town council to change Willow's fate.

The next day I waited for something to happen. I heard nothing. Another day went by with no news. Probably, I'd gone too far. Or maybe not far enough.

Chapter Thirteen

Broom in my hand, sweeping and scrubbing at dirt that had been tracked into the hardware store. It should be no surprise with all the workman frequenting the place.

I concentrated on the more obvious soiled areas not sure I made a difference. As I stopped to take a breath and scope out the progress, I glanced up to see Mr. Bennett gazing out through the front window. He turned to me with eyebrows drawn together. "Did you walk to work this morning? I don't see your car in the lot."

A day didn't go by that he failed to keep track of me.

"I'm in the lot behind the bank. The one located a block on the other side of The Caffeinated Cup. It's only a two-block walk from there to work. Or, if I want to stop for coffee, it's a block to The Caffeinated Cup and then a block from there to the hardware store."

My boss tipped his head and gave me a look, probably wondering if I'd lost my mind. "Why would you do that?" He tapped the window. "There are plenty of spaces in the lot right across the street."

I leaned the broom on the counter. This would take some explaining. "Clair came up with a plan to keep us in shape. Every winter we slack off on exercising simply because the weather changes and it's cold. She says we get wimpy by taking the car everywhere. We drive to work or to the store, then once we get there, we park as close as possible. The only exercise we get is the run from the car to the door."

I grabbed the broom and swept dirt into the dustpan, waiting until after dumping it into the dustbin to continue. "Look how much healthy workout we lose every day. So, Clair suggested parking farther away from work. We pick up all those extra steps, and we aren't going to freeze in only a block or two."

Mr. Bennett liked Clair. He might've argued with me, but I knew he would give the idea extra credit if I stamped her name on it. "Like I said, Clair's idea and it's a good one. I wasn't too enthused about it at first, but it works, and I feel very adventurous. So, after work today I'll walk a block to The Caffeinated Cup and have my coffee. Then I'll walk another block to my car and drive home."

"What if it's snowing or sleeting when you get off?" My mother didn't even worry as much about my comfort as Mr. Bennett.

I smiled at him. "Thank you for your concern, Mr. Bennett, but I'll be fine."

"Hmm." My boss shrugged and walked into the storeroom.

~~

According to plan, after work I bundled up and hoofed it toward The Caffeinated Cup. Flakes of wet snow collected on my eyelashes. Coffee was only a block away, so I kept my head down and hurried toward the coffee shop. While anticipating the comfort of the hot latte, I almost ran into another woman stalking past me, also with her head down. I did a double take and skidded to a stop. "Ella? Is that you? I hardly recognized you outside the coffee shop. Did you finally get enough help that you can take time off? I'm just on my way to the shop now."

The woman stopped and raised her hand. I could see that it was Ella, but her cheeks glowed much pinker than usual and snow had built up in her hair. She stared blankly at me. As one of her best customers, I expected a greeting. Instead, stress lines crossed her forehead. I stuttered. "Um. Sorry to bother you. You must have a lot on your mind." I tried to lighten the mood. "The only thing I'm concerned with is whether to get a latte or a caramel macchiato, today."

A flash of recognition lit her face. "Oh, Libby. I'm sorry. My mind was elsewhere." She paused for a deep breath. "You're right, I've taken the day off. But don't bother going to the shop. It's closed."

"Closed? Oh dear. What happened?" I wanted to sound concerned for her, when my thoughts flew in all directions. What would I do without The Caffeinated Cup? Where would Clair and I meet? It's my second home. "What's wrong? Don't tell me you're retiring."

Ella couldn't be old enough to retire. My heart raced. Is this what a panic attack felt like? I needed to call Clair and let her know. I needed someone to cry with me.

I took two deep breaths to readjust my attitude and tried to turn my focus on Ella instead of me. "Is it a health issue? Are you alright? Is The Caffeinated Cup really closed?"

Ella put up a hand and gave a rather sad smile.

"Take it easy, Libby. The Cup isn't closed forever. The doors are locked for today only. I'll be back at the helm tomorrow morning—whether I want to be there or not."

"That's a relief. What happened today? Damaged water pipe? Have you found a repairman?"

"No, not the pipes. More like damaged people. I'd had my fill and couldn't talk to one more petty customer. Every person who walked through the door this morning wanted to argue, but not about my coffee or my food. About the Willow Ottenweller case.

"I want all my customers to feel at home. Like family. The trouble with family is that they bicker like children."

Ella rolled her eyes and snugged her arms across her thick coat before continuing. "Seems like everyone had coffee with a side of hate. Everyone! I went to top off everyone's coffee, thought I'd give them an extra treat. But I didn't find one pleasant conversation. They're taking sides and forming gangs. Either they think Willow's innocent or she is guilty. Oh, and there's even a bunch who think she did it, but was justified and should be congratulated."

Ella ran her hands through her hair to brush off some snowflakes. "I thought if I could only make it through the morning rush, I'd be okay. And I got through it without losing my cool. But then the lunch crowd arrived. Same thing. Enough of the cackling and quarrelling. I decided, right then, to close up. Went around and told every table to go home. If they hadn't finished eating, I handed them a doggy bag and sent them out."

I shoved my hands in my pockets and pulled my coat closer. I'd begun to shiver. "The Caffeinated Cup is my favorite place, mostly because of the homey atmosphere. It's hard for me to believe anyone could behave so badly, and I sure can't blame you for shutting it down. Though I was looking forward to it today."

She took a deep breath of the frosty air and stared out at the traffic. "The Caffeinate Cup has always been a peaceful place. A haven away from the rest of the world. For twenty years I've looked forward to going to work. It's been my pleasure to provide a place to relax, enjoy coffee, and enjoy friendship. But today, the Caffeinated Cup family turned into a bunch of hateful teenagers. They showed no grace in listening to differing opinions."

Ella pulled her handbag over her shoulder and began to breathe normally. "Maybe by tomorrow they'll be over it and behave better. Maybe they'll even apologize, though I won't hold my breath. I'm going home to take a nap."

Ella stepped away then stopped and twisted toward me. "And another thing. Just before I locked the door, Oscar White turned up to check on the petition he'd left there. Boy, that was poor timing. I blew up and told him I wouldn't show that thing to anyone and never try to involve me in it again. He kept his mouth shut and stomped out. Thankfully, he took the petition with him." Ella turned the corner and strode toward the parking lot where she always stowed her car.

I stood for a moment, feeling more sorry for myself than for Ella. No latte macchiato. I trudged on, trying to remember where I'd parked my car.

I found Ella's story hard to believe. But she had no reason to exaggerate. If she wanted a break, she could close The Caffeinated Cup anytime. I passed the shop with the glaring closed sign on the door. About half a block farther on, I came up to a cluster of people huddled on the sidewalk. Steam rose from the center of the group as they engaged in heated discussion. I took the opportunity to hear the complaints for myself and eased into the outside edge of the crowd. Oscar White stood in the group, surprisingly quiet in the midst of the ranting. After a few minutes he dipped his head, backed out of the group and hustled away. I listened to the others.

A woman with unnaturally dark hair, whose name I couldn't remember—my mother would—said, "It hurts my heart. The thought of that sweet lady being in prison. Oh sure, I believe she killed Harley Ottenweller, but I don't blame her."

A white-haired woman pointed toward the sky. "It's the law. You can't kill people, willy-nilly, simply because you don't like them. She deserves prison."

A man's voice rang out. "Hold on. They don't even know for certain that the bones belonged to Harley Ottenweller. Maybe it was someone else."

The white-haired woman retorted. "For gosh sakes, you think someone else died on Ottenweller property and happened to have Harley's identification on him?"

"Maybe they're the bones of a thief who stole Harley's wallet." The man's voice faded out as he probably saw a flaw in his reasoning.

Sheila, petite and longhaired owner of the local candle shop, spoke next. "I heard the bones were huge. Probably Bigfoot bones. The police have them hidden because they don't want to start a panic."

I jumped at a shout blasting from behind me. "Not that Bigfoot crap again. There's no such thing.

Government started that rumor to keep everyone afraid. It's their way of controlling the masses."

The white-haired lady again. "This is all ridiculous. Willow Ottenweller confessed. We know she did it and she should be put away. Should have been long ago. The case has drug out far too long. We don't want a murderer hanging around here."

I'd heard enough—more than I cared to—and backed away from the crowd. Things were getting out-of-hand in this town. I couldn't get home fast enough.

~~

I shed my work clothes and put on baggy jeans and a sweatshirt, then went straight to the kitchen and popped a bowl of popcorn. With the house to myself, I got cozy on the sofa and found a movie I hadn't seen. The flick was about to begin when I heard the front door creak open and slam shut. I put the popcorn down and started to get up to investigate when Mom came trotting into the room.

My mother stood over me with her hands on her hips. "I'm disgusted. People are fighting all over town, even at the library. I'd stopped in to look for a book on detective work." She grinned and showed me the book in her hand. "I found this. Tips on Being a Master Detective. Can't wait to read it. Won't Jack be surprised?"

I didn't think that required an answer and waited for her to get back on topic.

Mom took the hint. "Well anyway, Lucille—she's the librarian now—said the police should get on with it and send Willow away. Lucille says we all should come to terms with the facts. She's a coldblooded murderer who killed her husband. Otherwise, why has she stuck to her confession so long? And Lucille said she'd heard that Willow never even cried when she confessed."

Mom paused. "You know, I hadn't thought of it before, but it's true. She didn't cry. But not all women are criers."

Hugging her book to her chest, Mom sighed. "Personally, I still find it hard to believe Willow's capable of the hurting anyone. Of course, I realize she had a much different life than I had. She found herself in a very difficult marriage. I was blessed when I married your father. He was always respectful of me. Gerald and I talked about everything, made decisions together. There was never a time when I didn't trust him completely."

At the door to her room, Mom rested her hand on the doorknob. "Wait to start the movie. As soon as I change, I'll join you. It will be good to have something to take our minds off poor Willow."

Chapter Fourteen

My mother stood at the window wearing her robe and slippers. She cradled her evening cup of tea. "The wind brought down the last of the leaves. We'll need to get out and rake this weekend."

"Um. Maybe I can get Jimmy from the hardware store to come over. He's always looking for ways to earn money."

"Whatever you think. I don't mind paying him if he wants the work." She stretched to scan the street. "He could pick up some more jobs if he came over early. Everyone will be out cleaning their yards."

After dinner Mom retired to the living room to watch the news but turned it off after a couple of minutes. "I don't want to hear any more police business. After all that time we spent at the station. And the worry about Willow. I need an escape." She picked up a book and settled into the deep cushions of the sofa.

"Escape sounds good. I'll be going for a walk." I pulled a jacket from the closet and set off. After hopping down the porch steps I cut through the yard. Leaves crackled beneath my feet like the breakfast cereal. Snap, crackle, pop… scrunch. Loving the autumn leaves. Something I couldn't imagine ever growing out of. Playing in the fallen leaves brought memories of pure childish joy. A cool evening and fresh air, dark enough to have chased everyone else off the streets. No one around to wonder at the grown woman doing nothing more than hopping into the leaf piles.

Like Mom said, these leaves were destined to be raked up and carted away by the weekend. Winter drew ever closer and snow always dampened my enthusiasm for late night walks. I had grown out of my enthusiasm for snow play. I made no snowmen nor angels in the snow.

This night held the perfect combination of crisp, fresh air and dry leaves that had only been partially raked. I could crush them under foot and send them sailing with a kick.

So, I searched out little leaf piles on my stroll, listening to the crunch with each step. I took three steps listening to crunch, crunch, crunch. Two more steps, crunch, crunch, crackle. Hmm, that was strange. Sounded like I got a bonus with that step. I stood still. No more crunching. I marched on, in my blissful childish daydream.

Unexplained leaf noise stopped me in my tracks. Crunching that didn't originate with me. I whirled, scoping out the sidewalk and the yards behind me lit only by street lights. I found no one. Creatures other than people could crush dried leaves. There were squirrels and birds and rabbits scurrying about in the dark, going about their lives.

Silly me. Recent events had marred my peace of mind. I strolled on in search of the next pile. But the errant noise came again. The sound of smashed dry leaves followed me. I skidded to a stop and twisted quickly to the right, hoping for a glimpse of the ornery someone playing a trick on me. No one in sight. I shouted. "Who's there?" Waited for an answer, but none came. I walked on, determined not be afraid of the night in my little village of Twin Fawn. The sound of crackling leaves came in a rhythm without regard to where I placed my feet.

After taking a few more steps, I stopped and spun to the left, certain I would catch the jerk who wanted to terrify me. Again, there was no one there. Standing still, I listened. Something or someone pushed through the bushes. I took a deep breath and told myself to stop imagining things. It was a squirrel or a dog or something out to enjoy an evening stroll, just as I was.

Willow's stories came to mind. I talked to myself – silently, lest any neighbor hear me and realize I'd seriously lost my mind.

"Bigfoot or Sasquatch, or the Crosley Monsters are not real! Simply folklore. The stuff of children's stories and scary tales around the campfire." No matter that others believed. I would not be gullible.

"Tall tales will not spoil my evening walk!" Sadly, the fresh sweetness of the stroll had melted away, so I turned the corner and headed home. Many of the houses on my street were already dark. No porch lights on. Few lights inside save a flickering television here or there. Did everyone in this town go to bed early? If I called out, would anyone hear me?

Guess I'd been watching too many scary movies, and I'd let Willow's imagining—and Clair's—invade my thoughts. Now that made me angry. My favorite pastime ruined.

Stepping up the pace, the security of my house soon came into view. A short jog covered the final half block. Up the steps, unlocked the door, and with a final glance over my shoulder, I'd reached safety. This time that final glance caught something lurking in the dark. Had I imagined it? A shadow moved through the trees from my landscaping to the yard next door. It was big and sort of furry-looking. I didn't bother silencing my voice when I commanded. "Liberty Breeze Cassell! Straighten up. Stop imagining things!"

Once inside, I snapped the bolt into place and breathed relief. A glance at my mother's closed bedroom door told me she was likely catching up on sleep. She's a busy lady. Just as well. I didn't care to be laughed at for being afraid of the dark. Or worse, she might insist on accompanying me on my nightly strolls.

Still jittery after bundling up in my pajamas and robe, I peeked out the windows and pulled all the curtains. A cup of hot chocolate helped to settle my nervous stomach. By the time I'd watched a non-threatening romantic movie I slipped into deep slumber.

~~

Nothing disturbed my sleep until a jarring early morning phone call. My friend and health advisor, Clair, invited me out for a morning jog. She's persuasive and I'm easily persuaded. I consented, but only to a vigorous walk, no jogging.

I'd become accustomed to her habits, so I got dressed and at the door ten minutes early. She arrived as expected—early—and we set off. As soon as she hit the sidewalk her pace accelerated to barely short of a jog. I determined to keep up and did for the first block as we raced around the early rising neighbors out raking leaves.

It didn't take long for me to pant a request to slow down a bit. Clair acquiesced and spun to face me, chatting while she walked backward. Such a show-off. I wondered, not for the first time, what kind of jet fuel this woman drank. I'd guzzled a cup of coffee but still waited for it to kick in.

Without missing a backward step, she began. "Guess what happened to me last night."

I puffed. "I'm not in a guessing mood. I can hardly breathe."

"I had a showing of a house a few blocks from here. They liked it and we finished well after dark. The client left while I locked up. On my way to the car, I heard weird thrashing noise and some grunting in the yard nearby. Sounded like something stumbling around in the dry leaves. I used the flashlight on my cell phone but it doesn't produce much light, so I didn't see anything."

I held my tongue until she finished, waiting to expose her little scheme. "Okay. Very funny. That's really smart, telling me you had the same experience I had. But I'm not falling for it. You followed me and made scary noises in the bushes. I want you to know you ruined my walk. I got so nervous I cut it short and went home."

Clair cocked her head. "Honestly, girlfriend, I don't know what you're talking about. I'm trying to tell you that I think Willow might have been right about the Crosley Monster. I think it's still in town."

I put on the brakes, planted my fists on my hips, and took time to tell Clair of my experience. "So, if you were trying to frighten me last night, tell me right now."

Clair put up both hands. "I promise I'm telling the truth. I didn't know you were out, but it sounds as if you ran into the same weirdness I did. And I don't mind telling you, I was freaked out."

Still doubtful, I glared at her. "You didn't act frightened when we talked about the Crosley Monster before."

"I know, but I hadn't run into it, then."

I took a breath and pondered Clair's story. "It had to have been some creep trying to scare us." Having said that, I realized my dwindling confidence in this theory. And thoughts of the big shadow hanging out in my yard returned.

One more attempt at the folklore defense. "There is no such thing as the Crosley Monster. It's a tall tale."

Clair stared at me. "I'd rather believe in Bigfoot than in a man following us. Because we don't have creeps stalking women in Twin Fawn. That's one of my selling points to families moving here. I'm always raving about how safe our town is."

"You tell them we don't have crime but maybe they should watch out for the big hairy monsters roaming the streets?"

Clair sighed. "Of course, I don't mention Sasquatch. They would think I'd lost my mind." She pivoted and resumed our walk. I trotted to catch up. What would I rather hear, if buying a house? There may be stalkers or keep an eye out for Bigfoot.

More to the point, who or what had been out in the dark, stalking us last night?

We kept up the pace and I followed Clair through town. There were few people out at the early hour. We'd reached The Caffeinated Cup when I begged her to stop so we could catch our breath. Clair still had plenty of steam but I needed a break.

As she waited for me to breathe, my friend grabbed my arm and whispered. "Look. I think that might be our Crosley Monster. I followed the direction of her gaze. Maximus Bailey climbed out of his pick-up and lumbered toward us.

"Of course." I wanted to laugh, remembering how he had unknowingly fooled me before. But would Maximus be the type to pull pranks? "But Maximus doesn't seem like the type to pull pranks."

"Those are the ones who are the best at spooking people."

As we prepared to greet Maximus, George Trainer walked out of the coffee shop and slapped him on the back. "Thanks for your help last night. I couldn't have done it without you. Riley is more than a terrier. He's a terror. I probably should go around and apologize to whoever has holes dug in their yard."

Maximus laughed. "I'm happy to help anytime. Needed the exercise last night."

I glanced at Clair. "It wasn't a prank but George and Maximus terrorized us."

Clair addressed the men. "You gentlemen scared us to death last night. We heard someone thrashing about in the dark."

Maximus shrugged. "Clumsy me. I'm sorry I scared you. We spent at least an hour chasing Riley through yards and cross-country."

"That's a relief. We didn't know what to think, with all the talk of the Crosley Monster. You must have been over on the north side of town near Bird Song Park. That's where I was when I heard you, and Libby was only a couple of blocks away, out for a walk. Both of us got spooked by something crashing about in the bushes"

I smiled at Maximus. "I didn't see Riley but you must have gone through my yard. I saw your shadow. And your sherpa coat makes you look so big." I laughed. "I thought Big Foot was after me."

George tipped his head and squinted at me. "North? No. Last night Riley took off for the southwest part of town. We weren't north at all." He glanced at Maximus. "Isn't that right?"

"Yes, sir. The little scamp took off running south and we followed him for blocks."

George turned to leave. "You ladies probably had a run-in with the real Crosley Monster. I can understand you having a fright. But no need to worry. Of all the newspaper accounts, there's never been a report of the creature killing anyone." George laughed and walked on down the street. Maximus gave a little three fingered wave and went into The Caffeinated Cup.

My best friend and I stood for a moment staring at each other.

"So, was it them, or not?"

"I don't want to think about it." Clair stepped out, continuing our power walk.

"Me either." I skipped a couple of steps to get in sync.

Chapter Fifteen

Clair and I were breezing through town in her BMW. I'd settled into her luxurious heated passenger seat when a large and anxious man caught my eye. "Slow down a minute. What's going on with Oscar White in front of the police station?"

Clair took her eyes off the road long enough to verify that Mr. White was in fact acting strangely. She gave me a sly smile. "Shall I stop so you can talk to him? I know you've been pining to help circulate that petition of his."

I cut my eyes to her. "Very funny. But watch him. He's pacing back and forth and flinging his arms. He looks like he's having an anxiety attack."

Clair pulled to the curb about half a block past Oscar and slid the gear shift into park. Then she twisted in her seat to watch. "He does seem to be agitated."

We both sat gazing out the back window studying Oscar's odd behavior. After a few minutes of watching the episode, guilt began to seep in. I kept telling myself I had no reason to feel guilty. But maybe I did. "Do you think he's alright? Maybe we should ask if he needs help."

"Are you a glutton for punishment? You know he'll

talk you to death about some new idea he has. Besides, he's right in front of the police station. If he needs help, it's the perfect place."

"I should talk to him. It looks like an anxiety issue and very few people will stop to help him. Most try not to look him in the eye for fear of getting pulled in to a conversation." I tugged at my seatbelt. "This thing is jammed."

"You're right. People won't stop—with good reason—he's not a likeable guy."

I glanced at Clair. "I feel sorry for him and I'm determined to be kind." I didn't tell Clair that I might have over-stepped by lying to Oscar. I continued tugging at the belt.

Clair kept an eye on Oscar while I struggled, then grabbed my arm. "Wait. Whatever it was must have passed. Looks like he's pulled himself together. He's stopped flailing about."

I gave up trying to free myself from the darn seatbelt, and glanced over my shoulder. Sure enough, Mr. White had straightened and marched down the sidewalk. "Oh, that looks good. I guess he's settled the problem himself."

"Are you satisfied that he's okay?"

"Yes. He seems to be stable."

Clair put the car into gear and pulled into traffic. "You really are too kind hearted. You worry about your mother, although she's pretty self-sufficient. You're stressed about Willow Ottenweller. The jury is still out on her mental state. Do you really want to add an elderly bully to the list?"

"Someone needs to care. But I know you're right. I can't fix everyone. I'm sure Mr. White is fine."

Clair pointed to the seatbelt latch. "By the way, did you forget you have to push the button on this side of the latch to release the seatbelt?"

~~

I'd finished my share of the kitchen clean-up duties after dinner and looked forward to retiring to my room to start reading the latest novel by my favorite suspense author. My mother had a movie she wanted Jack to see, so they were setting it up in the living room. I'd said goodnight and was on my way out of the living room when heavenly bells began to chime. This is what happened when I let my mother choose the new doorbell when we replaced the front door.

"I'll get it." I stepped to the entry way and pulled open the door, hoping to see my friend, Clair. As soon as I recognized Oscar White on the porch, I almost slammed it shut, but stopped myself. Questions flew through my mind. Had he discovered my deceit? Did he seem angry? How did he know where I lived? I answered that on soon enough. He'd only have to inquire of anyone in Twin Fawn. I stood gawking at him for a moment.

"Mr. White. This is a surprise." I stared at him for an awkward couple of beats as he stood with his hands in the pockets of his coat. After a mental shake to get my brain in gear I remembered my manners. "Step in out of the cold. What can I do for you?"

He took a few steps into the entryway and leaned to the left as if I was in his way. He gazed past me into the living room. "I'm not here to see you. I want to talk to Jack Reed. Heard he spent time at this address. Is he here?"

I sucked in a deep breath of relief. No

condemnation for my lies—yet. "Yes, he is. Come on in." At that point I dropped the formalities. He'd already passed me on the way to the living room.

As soon as my mother noticed we had company she hopped up out of her chair. "Good evening, Oscar. You have perfect timing. I just brewed a fresh pot of decaf. How do you like yours?"

He gave her a quick glance. "Uh, thank you. I take it black, not too strong." He quickly shifted his gaze to Jack and limped toward the empty recliner. "I'm glad I found you, Reed. You being an ex-cop. We need to talk. It's important."

"Sure. What can I do for you?" Jack waited for Oscar to settle into the recliner and took a seat on a chair next to him.

"I'll help you, Mom." I was dying to stay and listen, but figured that would be impolite since he'd singled out Jack. I followed my mother to the kitchen, but wasn't much help. She poured the coffee, and I hung back and leaned on the door frame to eavesdrop.

Oscar wasted no time. With his elbows on his knees and eyes on the floor, he said, "I want you to go down to the police station with me. I'm going to make a confession. I killed Harley Ottenweller."

"What?" I lost my balance and stumbled from the doorway into the hallway.

Oscar glanced at me as I steadied myself and then turned his eyes back to the floor. Jack, a very patient man, stayed silent.

Since I'd landed half-way back into the living room, I couldn't resist putting in my two cents. "Oscar, you are fond of Willow, that's obvious. But you won't be doing her any good by confessing to a murder you didn't commit. She's already admitted she did it."

Oscar raised his head and glared at me. "She didn't kill him. I did."

My mother chose that moment to arrive with the coffee. She nudged me out of the way and handed Oscar a mug. "Now, Oscar. Don't you want think about this? Why don't you drink your coffee and we'll talk about it. You know, down at the jail, they're taking good care of Willow. They understand that she's had a hard life. My friend, Elenore, she works down at the station, says Willow probably won't have to serve much time. Since she's old, maybe even get a suspended sentence."

I still needed to put my two cents in. "And Willow's happy. She's made her cell really cozy."

Jack raised a hand to silence us. "Katherine, Liberty, sit down and let me talk to Oscar."

We quietly made our way to the sofa and sat. We leaned toward Oscar. "Tell me the story. How did it happen?"

Oscar set his coffee on a side table and slumped back into the recliner.

"I've kept this a secret for years. I can admit it now. My feelings for Willow were strong back then. More than affection. Deep love, even when I was still married. Willow never returned the affection. She's a God-fearing woman. Stayed true to her husband even when he wasn't good to her."

He gazed into the distance. "In her younger days, you'd never seen a more beautiful woman. Certainly better than Harley Ottenweller deserved. The abusive jerk. I witnessed it myself. Verbal abuse—both toward Willow and to his son, Johnny. I figured it wouldn't be long before he would get physical. Someone needed to do something about it. Turns out, it would me who did something."

"I saw him on my way home after bowling league one night. It was late and I'd had a few beers. He stood out behind his house. There used to be a ravine at the back of his property, and he'd been doing some sort of work back there. It was late enough that there was no one around, so I decided to speak to him. At first, I tried to talk some sense into the man. Get him to appreciate what he had. He wasn't interested in what I had to say and even accused Willow of having an affair with me. Like I said, she would never do such a thing. That turned it into a shouting match. It got pretty darn heated."

Oscar paused to take a quick gulp of coffee. "I guess he'd been digging because there was a shovel laying on the ground. While we exchanged insults, he pushed me and I pushed him back. Then he struck me with his fist. He was a big guy so it set me back. I stumbled and fell to the ground. I reached out and grabbed the first thing I could lay my hand on. Well, the shovel was right there and the next thing I knew, I'd swung it at Harley."

Oscar took his napkin and wiped perspiration from his forehead. "Kind of shocked me when it made contact. Harley dropped like a stone. Straight to the ground. When I got up and looked, there was blood. I stood there and watched him but he didn't move. Then I knew he was dead, so I pushed him into the gulley and covered him with leaves and branches. I left him there. Thought maybe whoever found him would consider it an accident—which it was, really. I went home and tried to forget about it."

Oscar looked at Jack. "I didn't know what else to do."

Jack nodded. "I understand that. But then what happened? They didn't find Harley in the ravine."

Oscar took a deep breath. "A couple days later Johnny started that gazebo. I saw him in the yard and asked what he was doing with all the wood and the tools. He said his dad hadn't come home and his mom was sad, so he wanted to do something to make her feel better. I told him what a good son he was, and I wanted to help him." Oscar looked up and shrugged. "Sure didn't want the kid to find Harley's dead body there in the gulley. So, I knew I'd have to do something with him. After that first day's work, Johnny had left boards strewn around the yard and dirt piles from digging the foundation."

Oscar put up an index finger and tapped himself on the head. "That's when I got the idea. I snuck back in the middle of the night and dragged the body out of the ravine and across the yard, all the way to the house. I told you he was a big guy. It took a while, but I got him there. Then, I buried Harley right there behind the house, under one of the dirt piles."

I'd been quiet, sitting on the edge of the couch, even complimenting myself for letting Jack take the lead. But Jack hadn't asked the question that bothered me. I leaned in and spoke casually, as if inquiring about his coffee instead of a dead body. "I don't understand why you chose a location so close to the house. Would you explain your thinking on that?"

Oscar almost smiled at his answer. "I told you about the dirt piled up in different parts of the yard, so we—I—figured no one would notice the ground had been disturbed if I dug deep enough. We—no, I—dragged Harley up there and buried him." He shook his head. "Sorry, I'm not thinking straight."

Jack slid his chair a little closer to Oscar. "You said we, instead of I, and corrected it twice. You're a smart man. I think you've got it straight, and at least subconsciously, you want to tell the truth. Someone helped you. Isn't that right? Who helped you bury Harley?"

Oscar shook his head and stared into space. "Nobody. Just me. I misspoke. This is all so upsetting and I'm an old man." He got up and paced to the window. The glass steamed up from his breath as he stared outside. "I did it alone."

He'd obviously lied, and I wanted to tell him so. I had a sinking feeling I knew who had been with him that night. Who else could it be but Johnny? Willow would be heartbroken to see her son go to jail.

Chapter Sixteen

Oscar returned and crumpled into the recliner. He leaned back, face pale, eyes dull and nearly closed. The man looked completely drained. I thought he might not get up again.

After a few quiet minutes, Jack stood and put a hand on Oscar's shoulder. "Let's go down to the station. You've already learned you can't ignore the truth. Let's not put it off any longer. There's no sense in spending another day worrying about it." Not waiting for a response, Jack walked to the closet and pulled out his jacket. After a couple beats, Oscar pushed himself up from the recliner and shuffled behind Jack. My mother ran for her coat, and I scurried after her. We bolted for the door after the men stepped out.

Oscar climbed into the passenger seat of Jack's car, but Jack stood beside the front bumper waiting for us. "We'll drive two cars. I'll take Oscar. I want to talk to him on the way."

"But, I…" Mom closed her mouth, reached into her handbag, and pulled out her keys. "Liberty and I will meet you there."

I stared at her for a moment, still waiting for the outburst. Mom had to be dying to hear what they talked about. But she obediently climbed into her own car. I followed suit, taking the passenger seat.

My oddly quiet mother drove to the station. Possibly her teeth were still clenched after receiving an order from Jack.

The silence was killing me. I needed to talk and filled the time with questions. "Do you believe Oscar? I'm wondering if he made it all up. But I don't know why he would. Unless he's really still in love with Willow."

She simply nodded and hummed a 'yes' or maybe an 'I don't know' while keeping her eyes on the road.

I kept talking. "I guess his confession is easier to believe than Willow's. But I can't figure out why she stuck to her story all this time."

Mom's eyes remained on the road. "I can only guess at Willow's motives. It baffles me that Oscar waited all this time to confess to the murder. I wonder what prompted him."

I almost blurted out my own confession, but kept quiet as she went on.

She finally glanced at me. "I don't believe that sweet little woman could kill anyone. What I do believe is that she'd give her life to protect someone else. Someone she loved. And I don't think that person is Oscar White."

Mom and I entered the police station just as Jack announced the purpose of their arrival. Several police officers stopped what they were doing and stared at us. Arnie came from his office. "What? Another confession? Is this a joke?"

He studied the seriousness of Jack's expression. "Okay. No joke." Arnie stepped back and opened the door to the interview room. Oscar and Jack walked in immediately taking seats. Arnie was about to shut the door in our faces when my mother stuck her foot out and insisted that we be allowed to join them. She almost always gets her way. We slipped past the officer.

Twin Fawn P.D. has only one interview room. The station isn't very big, so the room may also double as their lunchroom. It smelled a bit like hamburgers and fries. In any case, we sat in the same cold, flat gray room where Willow had spent hours after the discovery of Harley's bones. Furnishings consisted of one rectangular table and four folding chairs–Arnie had to pull in one more to seat all five of us. There were no windows except the one in the door opening to the hall way and front desk area.

We all listened to Oscar's story again as he told it to Arnie. Finally, the officer nodded, "Okay" and left the room. Within a minute he'd returned with paper and pen that he handed to Oscar, who painstakingly recorded the details of the story he'd related. A confession to Harley Ottenweller's death.

Arnie leaned back in his chair and stretched his legs out to the side. "That's quite a story. I must admit it's a lot more believable than Mrs. Ottenweller's confession. Let's bring her in and see what she says."

Arnie had Willow brought in as well as another folding chair. After hearing Oscar's confession, she tipped her head and stared at him for a moment. "You killed my husband?"

Oscar gazed at her with a trembling frown and hauntingly sad eyes. "I did. I'm so sorry, but I couldn't let him treat you that way anymore." He held her gaze. "I didn't set out to kill him. But I wouldn't have been a man if I'd ignored his behavior."

Willow turned to me. "I knew Harley was dead. Could just feel it in my being. But I blamed Johnny." She slowly shook her head and put her hands over her face. "All this time I considered my boy capable of murder."

As she dropped her hands, I could see the tears forming. "As soon as he began work on the gazebo, I thought, 'he's hiding Harley's body'. But my son really didn't kill his father. It's such a relief. Johnny is innocent."

Willow wiped her eyes and continued. "And then that dog found Harley's bones. I probably shouldn't have left dog food outside." She paused and lifted her shoulders. "I couldn't figure out why Harley'd been buried up next the house."

Turning, she pointed an index finger at Oscar. "I confessed to keep my Johnny out of jail. I thought I was protecting my boy and all this time it was you."

Willow twisted to gaze at me. Her eyes had brightened, and I could almost see dimples at the corners of her mouth. "And I've been guarding that darn gazebo with my life. Hallelujah, let them tear the thing down."

She sat up straight and smiled at Arnie. "Officer, I retract my confession. May I go home now? I have house plants that need watering."

Arnie ran his hands over his head, weaving fingers through sparse strands of hair. "Yes, you may. I've been trying to get you to go home since the first day you checked in."

The officer stepped to the door and called into the hallway. "Somebody escort Mrs. Ottenweller back to her cell and help her collect her things. Better grab a box. She has a lot of stuff in there."

The little woman nearly bounced from the room.

After he shut the door, Arnie asked Oscar to repeat his testimony, one more time, double-checking everything with the written copy.

As Oscar came to the end of his testimony, Arnie nodded. "Got it. That's everything."

"Wait." Jack held up a hand. "Officer, we're not done"

Jack turned to Oscar. "I don't think you're finished, are you, Oscar? I've been sitting here expecting to hear the whole truth. You remember that the first time we heard the story, you made a couple of mistakes that indicated you may not have acted alone. I believe you had help in disposing of Harley's body. You couldn't have handled burying Harley by yourself. It's time you told Officer Arnie who helped you."

Oscar's wide eyes reminded me of caged tigers at the zoo. All the more so, when he got up and paced around the table.

We watched his course through the room, waiting for an answer. After a few minutes, Oscar stopped and turned toward us. "I carry the bulk of the blame. Adding to the story won't change a thing. But I'll tell you, now."

My heart sank. I thought of poor Willow and how heartbroken she'd be. But it was best to get it over with. Still, Oscar stood mute as if he couldn't bring himself to finish his confession.

My mother's favorite quotation, 'The truth will set you free.' ran through my mind. The truth often tended to be painful at first, but it had to be told, and I couldn't wait for Oscar White any longer. I blurted the answer. "It was Johnny, wasn't it? He helped you bury Harley. Did he help you kill him, as well? Nobody would have blamed him. He'd witnessed Harley's abuse of his mother and received it himself."

Oscar propped his hands on the back of his chair and focused on me. "What? No. Not Johnny. He wasn't there and didn't know anything about it." He ambled around the chair and eased into it.

He took a deep breath and let it out. "It was the mailman. A man by the name of Cassell."

I grabbed the table to keep from slipping off my chair. "What?"

My mother jumped up and screeched. "That's ridiculous. I thought you said you wanted to tell the truth. Now, I know you're lying. Why would you make up such a terrible thing?"

Jack reached out and took Mom's hand. "Wait. Let's hear him out."

Most people know better than to tangle with my mom. "No. I won't let him say that about my husband. Gerald's not here to defend himself, but I'm here." At this point I could almost imagine my mother forming fists and beating her chest.

Was I in the middle of a dream? A nightmare? Didn't Oscar White realize who he spoke to? We were the only Cassells in Twin Fawn. My father had been Twin Fawn's beloved mailman for many years before a massive heart attack took him from us.

Jack, the voice of reason, urged my mother to sit down and listen to Oscar. Surprisingly, she returned to her chair and remained silent, at least for the time being.

I tried to take a cue from Jack and calm myself, though accusations against my father had my head spinning.

Jack spoke quietly. "Finish your story, Oscar."

"As I told you, I couldn't leave Ottenweller's body out in the gulley for Johnny to find. I went out in the early morning to drag Harley out of the ravine. Even as a young man, I've never been in good shape, so I wasn't making much progress. Before the sun came up, this mailman, on his early morning rounds, walked up and surprised me. He wanted to know why I was out there in the dark. I knew it wouldn't be long before he saw the body, so I had to tell him. I'm embarrassed to say, I was a mess. Crying like a baby. I spilled it all. About losing my temper, the fight. And about grabbing the shovel and swinging. That mailman turned out to be a real nice guy and believed me when I told him I didn't mean to do it. He agreed with me that Harley Ottenweller wasn't a guy many people would miss."

Jack glanced at my mother, whose breathing was coming hard and fast, but still controlling herself. He pressed Oscar. "I'm not sure we heard you correctly. Tell us the man's name again."

"I'll never forget him. He saved me that night. His name was Gerald Cassell, and he understood that I hit Harley in the heat of the moment. We both agreed that I'd worsened the problem by not reporting the death right away. And since, out of fear, I'd hidden it, it made me look like a murderer. I told him about Johnny and how I couldn't let him find his dead father. Cassell and I talked about it and both of us decided where to put him. We agreed the pile of dirt would camouflage the grave. Cassell helped me dig the hole next to

Ottenweller's house and cover him up. Then we piled up dirt on top to make it look the same as it had. Later, I helped Willow plant a flower garden there.

Cassell and I made a vow to never talk about it again. And we never did. This is the first I've mentioned it to anybody."

"Lies." Mom couldn't keep quiet any longer. She sputtered. "Gerald Cassell was my husband. I'd have known if he'd been a part of this. We never kept secrets from one another."

Oscar's voice had lost its fight. "Now, look. I have no reason to lie. I've confessed. I'm guilty of killing Harley Ottenweller. Cassell won't be hurt by it. I saw in the paper where he died years back."

My mother sank into her chair and pressed a tissue to her eyes. "At least, I thought we didn't have secrets. How could he have known of Harley's death and never mentioned it to me?"

My brain still spun, and I stood up. "Gerald Cassell, the mailman, was my dad. Ask anyone. They'll tell you, you couldn't find a more honest man."

Jack leaned back in his chair. "I considered him my friend. I never would have guessed he could hide a crime. But I remember Gerald had a kind, compassionate heart. Always the first to forgive and to show mercy. Always quick to help someone in need. We didn't always agree. Sometimes I thought he could be too compassionate. Always wanted to see the good in people."

He focused his gaze on my mother and me, taking in the sternness in Mom's expression. "I'm sorry, Katherine, I believe Oscar."

She gasped and turned away from Jack. "How

could you even think such a thing?"

The words came to my mind but I couldn't say them out loud. I agreed with Jack. For some reason the story rang true. It may have been the wrong move, but Dad would have had mercy on Oscar. If he vowed to keep the secret, he wouldn't even have told my mother.

My father was a good man. I'd get over his deceit—eventually. My mother knew her husband well, so I figured she'd think about it and after a while, agree. But she'd have to come to it on her own terms.

We sat quietly. No one had anything else to say. Finally, Arnie got to his feet, took Oscar into custody, and we filed from the room. Jack got into his car and drove away. I told my mother I wanted to walk home on my own, as I needed to clear my head.

Before she climbed into her car, she took my hand. "I believe your father would have had mercy on Oscar. I think he reacted just as Oscar said. Afterall, he forgave me many things during our marriage."

She got into her car and turned the ignition. "I'll see you at home."

I set out to walk home but cut through the park to take a last look at Willow's house before the demolition began.

I studied, not only Willow's mansion, but other homes on the street. If my father, a mailman who wouldn't even jaywalk, could help to bury a body in the middle of the night and then, keep it a secret for years, who could I trust? What other secrets were hidden in my town?

It would take time and many long walks to get over this chapter of life.

~~

My walk, long and peaceful, helped me to come to terms with the shocking information about my father. Later, at home, I dug a little deeper.

Mom sat in the living room. I stood leaning on the door frame. "Mom, did you ever have any suspicion that Dad knew more about Harley's disappearance than he let on? Even a fleeting thought? Was there ever anything that didn't ring true?"

When she looked up, my mother's eyes were tired. I saw no trace of her beautiful ever-present smile. "I've searched my memory. In fact, that's all I've been thinking about. But I never saw anything in your father that would lead me to believe he knew anything about Harley's disappearance."

I crossed my arms over my chest. "I don't understand it. Dad was the most honest person I'd ever met, next to you."

At this point my mother did smile. "There's your answer. You said 'Next to me.' Don't you remember the secrets I told you? In my youth, I wasn't an honest person. I reformed and put the past out of my mind. But I never admitted the truth until I had no other choice. If Gerald had known who I'd been before, I think he would have forgiven me, but I never took the chance.

"Your father had a reason for keeping his secret. My guess is that Oscar touched Gerald's heart. I'm not saying it was right, but Gerald did what he needed to do in that situation."

I tried to picture my father as he was at the time of the death. A man working to support a young family. "It's frustrating that we'll never know the whole truth. Do you think if he hadn't died of that heart attack, he would have told you, eventually?"

"Liberty Breeze, he took his secret to the grave and it's no use wondering about it now."

I could see my mother had had enough of my interrogation. I pushed away from the doorway and walked to the kitchen. "I'm going to ask him when I see him in heaven. It's my turn to wash dishes."

I got busy scraping plates and loading the dishwasher. After hand washing the pots and pans, I hung the dish towel on the cabinet and took another glance outside. "It's a nice night. I'm going to sit on the porch." I grabbed my coat and a knitted hat to pull over my ears. I turned back and picked up my cell phone and stuck it in my pocket.

I wanted to sit and think for a while, but I also wanted to talk to Clair. I didn't really want my mother listening in. Not that she would care, but you have to pick up privacy when you can get it when your roommate is your mother.

Mom snuggled into the sofa, and I suspected she wouldn't be awake when I came back in. "See you in the morning."

As the cool air hit my face, new energy pumped through my veins. I could release all questions of the past. No more worry about my friend Willow. My mother grew closer to forgiving my father for his secret. Nothing weighing me down.

Except the thought that there may be more secrets in this town.

Chapter Seventeen

Heavy wool coat buttoned up, knit hat pulled down over my ears, I called to my boss. "See you tomorrow. I'll grab the trash on my way out and take it to the dumpster."

If Mr. Bennett thought the offer odd, he gave no indication. "Thanks Libby. I appreciate it. Have a nice afternoon."

I hadn't made my plans known to Mr. Bennett. If he'd guess I'd be cutting through alleyways to the parking lot where I'd left my car, I'd be in for a lecture, expounding on the possible dangers of such a venture. I'd have to remind him that my trip wasn't through some shady city ghetto. We lived in Twin Fawn and it was broad daylight. The Harley Ottenweller—Oscar White excitement had faded, and life had returned to the mundane. I'd become bored with traveling the same two and a half blocks to my car every day. How quickly the novelty faded.

I struck out, imagining the interesting raw scenery while traveling past dark back doors and barren walls—embellished with graffiti. Some of our graffiti artists showed talent. It made up for the lack of decorated store windows, welcome signs and shop keepers posing with their best foot forward.

I knew there would be garbage cans, a lot of dirt, and maybe rats. Not so exciting, but I hadn't explored Twin Fawn's alleyways since middle school. Even if the alleys didn't prove as enticing as my memories, the adventure would offer a change of pace, and fresh scenery, if not particularly attractive.

I dumped the trash in the hardware store dumpster and walked half a block in the direction of the parking lot, sidestepping cans and bottles, and bits of debris tossed carelessly in the general direction of the trash cans.

I admit feeling like a kid again browsing the backs of the buildings, private parking spaces and dumpsters, with no one in the alley except me.

My first venture came in the form of a short lane cutting off to the left of the main alley. I skipped into it. After about ten minutes I'd taken two more turns and wished I'd chosen a brighter day. Heavy clouds hid the sun and shrouded each passageway in dreary—and spooky—shadows. I'd decided that when I reached the back door of The Caffeinated Cup, I'd pop in, surprise Ella, and have a cup of coffee. Unfortunately, I never found The Caffeinated Cup.

I kept walking and eventually made a turn I thought would lead to my parking lot. I was mistaken. How could anyone become so disoriented in a town they'd grown up in? I'd answer that question later, if I ever made it out of the maze I'd gotten myself into.

Another question I pondered while I trudged along. Why didn't the stores put names on their back doors instead of numbers? I'd never paid attention to the

Bennett's Hardware number so had no point of reference.

Cutting down another short alley, a steady flow of traffic came into view, signaling I'd found Main Street. Confident of my direction, I reversed and chose an alley that ran parallel. That route would surely lead me to my parking lot.

A loud clanging noise blasted down the alleyway and rang in my ears. I skidded to a stop and squinted into the dim light. A short distance ahead, a figure stood at a dumpster, having thrown back the lid. I retreated to the side of the alley, out of sight and planned how to explain why I—a grown woman—wandered the alleys. Reliving my youth wasn't the excuse I wanted to confess.

Then, I heard the voice of the last person I wanted to see on my trek. I'd arrived at the back of Twin Fawn's only dress shop, and Lovey Henderson stood at an open door.

I backed up and scrunched closer to the wall. Hiding in the shadows, along with spiders and other bugs, hadn't been part of my dream for the day, but I wasn't about to make my presence known to Lovey.

The man at the dumpster was Mr. Henderson, Lovey's father. He gave a package a shove into the dumpster and turned to Lovey. "Hey Baby. I'm getting rid of it, just like you wanted."

Lovey's whiney voice had always set my nerves on edge. "Daddy, it's about time you threw that ugly thing away. It was taking up space in the storeroom and I lived in fear that someone would walk into the store and see it. They might think we actually carried such a tacky garment in our inventory."

Her father leaned with one arm on the dumpster. "Awe, it wouldn't be so bad to stock clothing the working class might wear."

Lovey gave a little gasp. "Never. There are other stores for those people."

"I know. But at least this sherpa served its purpose. In fact, a dual purpose. Fred, down at the Tractor Supply was sure glad to get rid of it. He was so grateful he gave me a discount on it. He said he'd ordered two and they both came in extra-large. One of them sold right away but he thought he'd never get rid of the last one."

"I hope he didn't tell anyone you bought it. He wouldn't, would he?"

"Don't worry about it honey. We don't travel in the same circles."

Lovey stood silhouetted in the doorway. "You had a great idea, Daddy. I'm sure your Big Foot act had a lot to do with scaring that old woman into selling her property. And her stories about the monster closed the deal. They were perfect for convincing the town of her unstable mental state."

Mr. Henderson leaned into the dumpster and gave the garbage bag one more shove. Another clang rang out as he closed the lid. "I almost hate to throw away the ugly thing. It's the warmest coat I've ever worn."

"Eewww. Better to freeze than to be seen in something like that."

I almost choked in an effort not to scream. It was all I could do to keep quiet when I heard their mean scheme. As soon as Lovey and her father retreated inside the dress shop and shut the door, I took off at a trot toward my car and home.

~~

"Mom, you'll never believe it!" My mother sat at the table while I ranted and spewed the whole story of Mr. Henderson's treachery. I stomped from the living room to the kitchen, waving my arms. I stomped back demanding, "I'm reporting them to the police. They both should be arrested."

My mother remained calm until I'd quit yelling. "It was a mean thing to do, but I doubt he did anything he could be arrested for. And think about it, we've just been through the whole Harley Ottenweller murder thing. Everyone is tired of the stress."

I'd run out of steam and sat across from my mother at the table.

She continued. "Willow is happy in her new home. She has enough money from the sale of her house to support herself for the rest of her life. I agree it was terribly wrong of Henderson to fool her into thinking the Crosley Monster roamed the streets of Twin Fawn. But we know that Willow is better off in the retirement village. And remember, she had some odd ideas about other things as well."

"I remember. I'll never look at a flower again without wondering if it might rebel."

Mom got up and went to the living room. "God takes care of sweet people like Willow. And He will deal with people like the Hendersons, in His timing."

I followed her and sank down into the recliner. "I know you're right. I only hope I'm around to see it."

~~

Business had been slow at Bennett's Hardware when Mom walked in a few days later. She rarely visited me at work. Most news could wait until I got home. But, on this day, she stood at the counter with a fist on her hip and tapping her toe.

I made my way around my desk and joined her. "What's up? With that Cheshire Cat grin on your face, it's obvious you have some good information for me."

"You'll never guess what happened."

I stared at her and waited.

She took the hint. "Yes, dear. I know you don't like to guess. So, I'll tell you. We thought the Willow Ottenweller case was over and done, didn't we?"

I nodded and wanted to beg her to get to the point. "Yes."

"There's been a strange turn of events."

I waited a beat before urging her along. "Everything about the case was strange. I don't think you can surprise me."

Mom unbuttoned her coat and unwound her knitted scarf. "Do you remember how Oscar White loved his petitions?"

"Sure. He almost had me carrying one around for signatures to get Willow out of jail."

"That wasn't his only document. He had another paper written up to declare Willow's house a historical site. We know, now, he only did it to keep people from digging around the property and finding Harley Ottenweller's remains."

"Yes. To keep his part in Harley's death a secret."

"Well, he didn't have much time to circulate that petition before they found the remains and everything blew up." Mom put her elbows on the counter and put up an index finger. "But a few people saw it. Someone had a copy and brought it to the attention of Twin Fawn's historical society."

"Wait a minute. Twin Fawn has a historical society?" This news took me by surprise.

My mother giggled. "Oh, we do. You would need to frequent the library to notice it. There's a little group of seven women who meet there twice a month. As far as I know, they've never done anything beneficial for the town, but they meet to gossip and read books on history. Well..." Mom put up a hand. "Not actually history books. The ladies read historical romance novels and discuss them at their meetings."

"So they call themselves the Historical Society instead of the Historical Romance Book Club."

"Yes. Gives them more credibility, don't you think?"

"So, did they sign Oscar's petition?"

"No, dear. That wouldn't have done any good after Oscar went to jail." She paused to let me catch up with her thought. "What they did is decide to activate. They put down their novels and went to see the mayor. I guess all seven walked right into his office. Once they got started, they probably talked his ear off." Mom took a moment to laugh. "But as a result, the mayor's decided to improve Twin Fawn's image by declaring the Willow Ottenweller house a historical landmark. And he agreed to turn it into the Twin Fawn History Center. Of course, the town will need to restore it first. The historical society ladies talked him into keeping Willow's plants to landscape the outside. They're even talking about putting up a plaque with Willow Ottenweller's name on it, thanking her for spending so many years caring for the place."

"That's sweet. Willow will be pleased."

"It's too bad there won't be much extra property

space to extend Bird Song Park. Someone on the city council wanted rose gardens and someone had mentioned a water feature. There won't be any of that, but what the mayor has in mind will be so much better for the town."

Chapter Eighteen

Clair navigated her black BMW around a pothole as she turned onto Main Street. "I heard your mom found some interesting information on the history of Twin Fawn."

On the passenger side, I turned up the seat warmer. "Yes, she told me she'd uncovered a few documents concerning the founders while she served as librarian and had tucked them away for safekeeping. She's been helping the new librarian locate them for the History Center. They'll have them framed and ready when the town has finished renovating Willow's house."

Clair tapped the steering wheel. "I never expected this turn of events. Isn't it exciting? Twin Fawn is more than a small town. It has history and its own History Center. This could develop into a tourist attraction. The whole town will benefit. I'll direct my clients over there. Prospective buyers love to hear about the history surrounding their new home."

"Mom said Loren Sanderson found some old documents in his attic about the building of the Main Street business area. She'll be going through them to decide which will fit into the center."

"What a boost for community spirit. People all

over town are going through their attics in search of treasures to add to the collection."

With a gust of wind, a few raindrops hit the windshield. Clair promptly turned on her windshield wipers and raised her eyebrows at me. "I knew it was going to rain. Told you to grab an umbrella, didn't I? That wool jacket you're wearing will soak up the water. You'll freeze."

I knew the weather tended to be unpredictable in Twin Fawn. Even seasoned forecasters had missed this approaching storm but Clair almost always predicted correctly. I'd stubbornly ignored her warning.

Clair pointed to a parking place directly across from The Caffeinated Cup. "I'll grab that spot. If we hurry, we'll get inside before the rain picks up." Distant thunder rumbled as Clair and I hopped out of her car. We trotted across the street to the coffee shop, dodging the scattered sprinkles.

I happily scooted inside the building with a barely damp coat and grinned at my friend. "By the time we're ready to leave, the storm will pass." Crossing my fingers.

"Uh Huh." Clair pulled off her faux fur lined rain coat. Where did she find that? With Twin Fawn's freaky weather, it might be worth the investment.

"Perfect." Clair marched to the table-for-two available beside the window. "My favorite pastime is holding a good cup of coffee while I watch the rain." We took our seats as the clouds thickened and the rumbles grew louder.

My friend peered out the window. "Don't you love that sound? So mysterious. It's like something exciting—or threatening—is on the horizon and creeping our way."

"I like the sound of distant thunder, but I've always thought of it as a warm cozy feeling. Something unknown approaching from the horizon is not exciting. It's scary." I watched dark gray clouds drift over Twin Fawn and waited for the deluge Clair anticipated. I couldn't help but let out a sigh. A soft, gentle shower would be more to my liking.

Clair rearranged the vines hanging from the pot suspended from the ceiling, while I went to the counter to collect our coffee.

Ella handed me the cups and bustled over to our table with scissors and a dish towel. "Sorry, Clair. These plants have gotten away from me." She trimmed the vines high enough to clear the tabletop, bundled them, and used the towel to wipe the table. "They must love the climate in here. Darn things are growing like crazy. We planted greenery to create a peaceful atmosphere in the shop but these things make more work for me. Can't have them taking over the tables."

Clair held the bundled vines while Ella cleaned. "The vines provide a nice atmosphere. It's too bad you have to cut them, but I hear pruning plants stimulates growth."

Ella carried the cuttings to the trash can and gave Clair an eyeroll that signaled she found no encouragement in the news. "Gosh. I don't want them to be healthier. I want the pesky sprouts to stay out of my customers' coffee. I'm afraid I'll be trimming them every week until winter is over. Then they go back to live with my aunt."

With a shiny table and fresh coffee, I took a minute to scan the coffee shop, smiling at customers I recognized. The few occupied tables held older Twin Fawn citizens I knew through my mother or as patrons of the hardware store. The approaching storm likely kept many away but these gathered for comfort. Or possibly to talk about the odd weather we were having.

Settling into my chair, I savored the warm glow of the brew and waited for the rain—until the coffee shop door flew open. I jerked my head to see who'd arrived and snapped my gaze back just as fast. I hissed at Clair. "Shoot. Now I see the threat on the horizon you were talking about. Lovey Henderson just stormed in."

Lovey rushed directly to a table at the back and tossed her pink umbrella to the floor. I kept my face turned away and prayed she wouldn't notice me. The last thing I wanted on this tranquil afternoon was Lovey Henderson's veiled criticism.

I needn't have worried. She wasn't interested in, if even aware of, anyone in the shop. Lovey sat with attention glued to the front door. Within a few minutes, Garrett came in and walked to the counter. After Ella fetched his order, he carried two cups to Lovey's table and kissed her on the cheek. As I kept a stealthy watch over the couple, I noticed Lovey failed to reciprocate the affection. She spoke to him, but I was unable to hear her—no matter how hard I tried.

Clair motioned toward the couple and stifled a giggle. "I don't want to be mean, but it looks like Lovey Henderson is having a bad day. That woman always acts as if her life is perfect and the rest of us scrape by in a sad, mundane existence. Right now, she sort of resembles an angry dragon."

I stole a quick glance to see the dragon face, then shifted in my seat and cut my eyes to the side in order to observe without being obvious. A few discernable bits of their conversation drifted through the coffee shop.

I whispered to Clair. "Sounds as if she is upset about something."

Clair, who stared straight at Lovey and Garrett, without shame, whispered, "She sure is. That whiny voice grates on my nerves and I expect her to breathe fire anytime now."

Lovey's voice grew louder. We no longer needed to strain to hear her side of the conversation. She nearly shouted. "Daddy told me he would get that monstrosity of a house torn down. He promised, but now he tells me he can't. Some silly thing about it being historical." She waved a hand as if shooing a fly. "It's a shack that will be there forever. I'll have to look at it every day." She paused to dab her eyes with a tissue. "And I'll never get my rose gardens."

Garrett kept his voice so low we couldn't hear it above the rain outside, but I suspected he said something designed to placate a toddler in the midst of a tantrum.

Lovey screeched in reply. "The Historical Society insists that since Willow Ottenweller never planted roses, they won't even consider adding any to the landscape. There won't be room anyway. They've decided to keep that rickety old gazebo. Why on earth would they disregard my plans for a beautiful city park in favor of the whims of a feeble old woman?"

From the corner of my eye, I watched Garrett scoot his chair closer to Lovey. I could only hear murmuring as he spoke to her again.

I leaned toward Clair and whispered. "Poor Garrett.

I feel like we're intruding by listening to them. Let's talk about something else."

Clair shrugged. "This is the best entertainment I've had in weeks." But she turned to watch the traffic outside our window. "The rain is really coming down. Strange for this time of year, don't you think?"

I sipped my coffee and made a determined effort to pay no attention to the row taking place at the back of The Caffeinated Cup. I busied myself by examining the newly cut hanging vines until a crash reverberated from the walls of the shop. In one swoop, Clair and I pivoted toward the sound.

Lovey's chair lay on its side against the wall. She stood glaring down at Garrett. His mouth hung open as he stared back at her. She screeched. "You're not even trying to understand." With that, she grabbed for her sparkly blue handbag but missed, causing it to skid across the table and onto the floor. Lovey gave another cry of frustration, tossed her long hair over a shoulder, and stomped through the room. We swiveled in our chairs to watch her stalk from the coffee shop.

Clair clasped my arm. "She forgot her umbrella. It's pouring down rain. The woman must be having a nervous breakdown if she's going out in it. Her hair will be ruined."

We slowly pivoted and returned our attention to Garrett. He pushed his chair back and slowly moved to upright and replace Lovey's seat. He then gathered their coffee cups and napkins, returning the cups to the counter and tossing the napkins into the trash. He stood for a moment gazing at their table, before returning to retrieve the little blue bag and pink umbrella. Without making eye contact with anyone in the coffee shop, he strode from the building. Once outside, Garrett popped open the umbrella and lengthened his stride to catch up with his hysterical and now soggy, girlfriend.

Clair twisted toward me. "What's wrong with that man? I'd have left that handbag and the umbrella on the floor until I finished my coffee. Then and only then, maybe I would've picked up her prissy handbag and umbrella and taken them to her." Clair paused and smiled at me. "Nope. I'd have left them here. A rhinestone encrusted baby blue purse and pink umbrella do nothing for his image."

"But...." It took me a couple of minutes to weigh possible responses. I generally follow Clair's advice on these things. She tends to be more worldly savvy. But this time I decided to strive for higher ground. "I think patience is a great quality in a man, don't you?"

My friend gazed at me for a moment. "Are you defending him? Liberty Breeze Cassell, you're a hopeless romantic. You always want to see the best in every situation. But I know if you take time to think about it, you'll agree you don't want someone who lets a self-centered little girl push him around."

I leaned back in my chair, crossed my arms, and thought about it. Would Garrett Reed and I last as a couple? Of course, this was all conjecture. Quite obviously the man adored Lovey Henderson. Certainly not open to a relationship with me. So maybe he saw qualities in her that were worth his patience and understanding.

If I was honest, I could list tendencies of my own that likely caused others to cringe. The longer I thought, the more peculiar citizens of Twin Fawn came to mind with similar idiosyncrasies. It seemed everyone had their own set of quirks—some stranger than others. Yet, I liked this little town. Like pieces of a jigsaw puzzle, everyone seemed to fit together to create our community. Maybe all anyone needed was one person with patience and understanding to help them find their place.

    I'd take time to sort through these deep thoughts and develop a case for my side before discussing it with Clair. But for now, since she still stared at me with judgmental eyebrows, I shrugged and turned to watch the raindrops coursing down the window glass.

The End

Would you like to Help the Author?

Do you love the quirky characters of Evelynton and Twin Fawn? Help others find my books.

Tell your friends about my novels.

Read my books where others can see.

Leave a review on Amazon.com and goodreads.com. It doesn't have to be long. Even a short note is an encouragement and makes it possible for me to keep writing.

Or send your review to me. I post it on my website.

Comment on my Facebook Author page or my Blog.

Born and raised in Northeastern Indiana, Lynne Waite Chapman is a lover of mystery and suspense, but most of all people. In September of 2016, she published her first cozy mystery. The debut novel Heart Strings—first in the Evelynton Murder series—was a 2016 semi-finalist in the American Christian Fiction Writers Association Genesis contest. The next three in the series, Heart Beat, Murderous Heart, and Caffeinated Murder continue the adventures of three friends in the small town Evelynton, Indiana.

Lynne Waite Chapman began her writing career with fifteen years of writing weekly non-fiction content for the BellaOnline.com Hair site, drawing on her thirty plus years as a hairdresser. Retiring the Hair site, she has spent the next fifteen years sharing her faith and penning weekly content for the BellaOnline.com Christian Living site.

She has been a regular contributor of devotions for several print publications and devotionals and has written articles for many church bulletins and newsletters. She has also contributed articles to numerous internet publications.

For more information about current and past writing projects visit Lynne at:
https://www.lynnechapman.com

Find her on Facebook at:
https://www.facebook.com/LynneWaiteChapmanAuthor

Follow her Amazon Author page:
http://www.amazon.com/author/lwchapman

GoodReads:
https://www.goodreads.com/LynneWaiteChapman

Follow her on Twitter:
@LWChapmanAuthor

Instagram:
https://www.instagram.com/lynnewaite/

Also by Lynne Waite Chapman

Evelynton Murder Series
Heart Strings
Heart Beat
Murderous Heart
Caffeinated Murder

Secrets of Twin Fawn
Secret Guilt

Book Links

Author page
https://www.amazon.com/author/lwchapman

Heart Strings
https://www.amazon.com/dp/1944203621

Heart Beat
https://www.amazon.com/dp/1946939250

Murderous Heart
https://www.amazon.com/dp/1792872259

Caffeinated Murder
https://www.amazon.com/gp/product/B087FVZGQC?notRedirectToSDP=1&ref_=dbs_mng_calw_3&storeType=ebooks

Secret Guilt
https://www.amazon.com/Secret-Guilt-Small-Town-Mystery-ebook/dp/B0B1XC4N2F

www.ingramcontent.com/pod-product-compliance
Lightning Source LLC
LaVergne TN
LVHW012020060526
838201LV00061B/4384